Praise for Delivering Christmas

'A wise, warm, festive delight.'
Alex Brown, author of *A Postcard from Capri*

'I absolutely loved it! It's gorgeously romantic and uplifting!'
Emily Kerr, author of *Her Fixer Upper*

'No one captures the heart like Liz Fenwick! A beautiful love story of new beginnings intertwined with the unbreakable familial ties of the past.'
Amanda Geard, author of *The Midnight House*

'...the perfect Christmas tale!'
Christina Courtenay, author of *Promise of the Runes*

'Romantic, evocative and beautifully described, this is Liz Fenwick's signature Cornish comfort in a perfect Christmas treat.'
Pernille Hughes, author of *Ten Years*

Also by Liz Fenwick

Delivering Christmas

A Novella

Liz Fenwick

EMF Press

First published in 2023 by EMF Press

www.lizfenwick.com

ISBN: 978-1-7384170-0-1

For Gwen whose friendship means the world to me. She also loves Christmas and Christmas films as much as I do.

Chapter One

Theo looked about the tidy sitting room with both pleasure and dismay. David, Natasha and baby Zach had left for their new home three days ago. Boatman's Cottage was now spotless, free of baby clutter, and it felt hopelessly empty. It had been a tight squeeze when David and Natasha moved in at the start of the pandemic lockdown in March 2020 after their property purchase fell through. Nearly two years with her adult son, his wife, and as of the last year, Zach, had been both wonderful and exceptionally challenging in what was basically a four-room cottage.

Theo straightened a cushion on the sofa and spied a small stuffed animal lurking behind it. Cat emerged from the kitchen.

'Was it you or Zach who put this there?' she asked the large Norwegian Forest cat, picking the small stuffed rabbit up.

Cat took a look, snaked through Theo's legs and disappeared out through the open front door without giving anything away. It was November but the day was bright and not too cold. Theo moved to the door and watched Cat meander down the path to the river then heard a 4x4 making its way up her drive.

The cavalry had arrived to save her from becoming too lost in her thoughts and missing the chaos of her family. She picked up her backpack, notebook and phone. A text from David flashed up with a picture of Zach sitting on the kitchen floor in their new home on the outskirts of Exeter. Her heart tightened. She missed the three of them but they weren't far away, and Boatman's really wasn't built for four people and more baby kit than a child had a right to. All that remained now at Boatman's was a travel cot and this one floppy-eared rabbit. She slipped the stuffed animal into her pocket before heading out to meet her assistant Tim.

'Morning. Looks like we have a great day for Christmas tree shopping,' he said.

Theo climbed into the battered vehicle. 'We do.'

'God, don't look so grim. It's not a funeral we're heading to!' He reached out and gave her hand a squeeze. 'Cheer up old thing. They're only in Exeter.'

'True.' She watched his handsome face light up with his smile. That smile always pushed away the shadows of sadness in his green eyes. Romantic love had a way of clouding your vision. Thankfully there was no risk of that happening to her at fifty-eight. She was safe even if she was a bit low at the moment. Romantic intrigue wouldn't solve anything.

Tim's company was the balm she needed. He had moved to Milton Abbot after his partner walked out on him for a younger man two years ago. Theo had met Tim on one of her floristry courses and had immediately seen his skill. For the past year when the pandemic allowed, he'd been at her side for weddings, celebrations and workshops. But this was his first Christmas working with her and he adored Christmas, as he reminded her constantly. His garish Christmas jumper was only an outward sign of what she imagined was going on inside.

'Now tell me about the clients,' he said as he navigated through the narrow lanes.

Theo opened the notebook. 'Well, the hotel of course, and Jeanette.'

'My dream woman.'

'She's nearly eighty and not your type.'

'Ah, but she might have tempted me in her day.' He smoothed his hair.

'You're incorrigible.' She grinned, envying his self-knowledge. Hard-earned she imagined.

'I am.' He turned out onto the main road and headed to the Christmas tree farm. 'Who else?'

'We have five house to dress fully so I will need thirty trees for those.' She ran her finger down the list of names. Each one of them had become a friend during her time here in the borderlands between Devon and Cornwall.

'Thirty?'

'For those clients, yes, but we'll need more for the hotel and family.'

'Let me call you Mrs Claus.' He raised an eyebrow.

'Funny, not,' she said, but she smiled nonetheless.

'And one for you and me,' he added. 'Must not neglect ourselves.'

'For you, yes.' Theo watched the blur of passing scenery. It changed so quickly from the lush Tamar Valley to the open moorland.

'Don't go all "bah humbug" on me. Why no tree?' He cast her a quick glance. 'Cutting your own near the cottage?'

'No point in decorating the cottage this year.' After last year's merry chaos she didn't have the heart for it.

'Theo Pascoe,' he chided. 'They did invite you.'

'I know, but I had Zach for his first Christmas and Natasha's parents barely saw him, so it's only fair that they have this one with him.' Theo also remembered Natasha's postpartum sulk that Zach's first Christmas hadn't been in their own home. Nothing Theo had done had been right, no matter what she had tried.

'Fair it may well be,' he paused, tapping the steering wheel.

'But it's as clear as day that you are suffering from empty nest syndrome.'

Theo made a face at Tim but she couldn't deny that she was feeling down. He pulled into the farm entrance, parked and turned to her.

'You love Christmas,' he said. 'Let's go and find some of your Christmas spirit.'

She drew a deep breath. Boatman's had been way too crowded with Natasha working from home and David painting. Then Zach arrived and they all focused on the squirming bundle of joy. The only one who hadn't been impressed was Cat until the feline discovered that she preferred baby mush to cat food. Then she never left Zach's side, always hopeful for dropped offerings.

The scent of the fir trees filled the air. If anything would make her feel Christmassy, this had all the ingredients. She slung her backpack on, clutched her notebook, and joined Tim. It was the twenty-second of November and now was the time to choose the trees for size, shape and the personal taste of her clients. But her feet were dragging, which she knew was unwarranted. All she had to do was focus on the task at hand.

The small shed, housing the office, was decked out with tinsel, and the scent of cinnamon filled the air. 'Hi Sam.' Theo leaned in and kissed the cheek of the older man. 'I think this will be a big year for you. People need to celebrate.'

'Hope so.' He looked heavenward. 'How many trees this year?'

'Forty in total.' She consulted the list, debating if she might need one more for her cousin Jeanette's house. Her mind wasn't on really Christmas. In truth she was trying to think of anything else, but here at the tree farm the walls were covered with charts and a countdown calendar. It must focus the mind. Something she could use. Thirty-three days until Christmas. Her schedule was sufficiently full so there would be little time to dwell on anything other than work, and this year that would be perfect.

'Make that forty-two trees.' Tim stepped forward with his hand outstretched. 'I'm Tim Kingston, Theo's assistant.'

'Good to meet you.' Sam shook his hand vigorously. 'It's not like Theo to miscount.'

'She's not planning on having a tree this year but she must.' Tim sent her a look. 'I need a small one for my cottage. I may be alone but I am not doing . . .' He stared at her. 'The Scrooge.'

'I'm not Scrooge. I'm just enjoying having a tidy house with everything in its rightful place.' She pursed her lips. 'I'm simply not decorating this year.'

Sam suppressed a grin. 'If you say so.' He reached into the drawer and pulled out a Father Christmas hat and a headband with elf ears on it. 'I think these might be needed.'

Theo rolled her eyes as Tim positioned the hat on her head then adorned himself with the pointed ears.

'Come on Santa, let's show some spirit!' He held out his arm and Theo batted it away, knocking a design from her notebook. Tim dove to retrieve it. 'That will teach you for beating up your employees.'

'I don't,' she huffed.

'True but that's not the point. I choose to be your chief dogs-body because you are wonderful and so bloody talented.' He adjusted her Santa hat. 'But I don't like this lost Theo.'

'I'll leave you two to resolve this one.' Sam handed Theo a bunch of bright pink ribbons. 'You know the drill.'

She took them. 'I do.'

Tim held out his arm again and she took it graciously this time. They walked through the trees with Tim humming 'Jingle Bells', but despite the jaunty tune, the heavenly scent and the blue skies above Theo couldn't find the spirit. Even if it snowed at this very moment she wouldn't feel Christmassy. It wasn't in her this year and she couldn't force it.

'That's it,' Tim said as they walked through the trees. 'You need a man.'

'I don't.' Theo coughed. 'That's the last thing I need.'

Tim stopped by a tree and waved his hand up and down as if he was on a game show. 'This one says Jeanette. It stands out from the crowd and goes its own way.'

The tree was distinctive, tall and spiky. 'You might be right on the tree but that is all.' She handed him a ribbon which he tied to a branch.

'Seriously you need a man, or maybe a woman.' He gave her a wink.

Theo stopped walking. 'I don't need a romance in my life. Tried it and failed. I am enough.'

They approached another tree. It was tall and balanced which would work well in the arched entrance to the stable yard at Abbotswood Hotel which sat just across the Tamar from Theo's cottage. The tree was slim enough that people could walk either side of it. She tied a ribbon on the branch and ticked off the stable yard on her list.

'You are enough,' he said. 'I am too and despite my rotten experience I *am* hopeful of finding another love *and* I want the same for you.'

'I definitely want you to find love.' Theo fixed her glance on the handsome man beside her. 'You're thirty-three but I'm fifty-eight. Romance and love are off my menu. I'll keep love in my life from family and friendship.'

'God, the ex burned you badly didn't he?'

'No, I was the fool with the choices I made.' Theo laughed bitterly.

'Men are bastards.' He huffed, his breath forming clouds in the cold air.

Theo looked at him hard, suppressing a smile.

'Well, not all of us.' He placed his hands on his hips.

'There's me, there's your David and Zach, and of course there's Hugo at the hotel.'

'All the key men in my life are divine.' She thrust her hand into her pocket. The small rabbit was there, soft and soothing.

'Especially your brother Martin, the priest.' Tim winked. 'Now, take that chap over there.' He pointed and Theo followed his glance. A tall well-built man with greying blond hair stood chatting to Sam. The man looked up and his blue eyes met hers. She froze and he smiled slowly acknowledging her glance. Theo turned and marched to the far end of the row of trees.

'Bloody hell woman.' Tim raced behind her. 'You liked the look of him and he liked you.'

'Nonsense.' She rubbed her sweaty palms on her jeans. She was acting like a teenager and what was worse she felt like one. 'Now let's get back to the task at hand. Trees, lots of them.'

'As you wish ma'am.' Tim bent at the waist with a flourish before taking her elbow and leading her to a tall shapely tree. 'For Toby, I think.' He pointed to Theo's great-uncle on the list. She wasn't dressing Toby's house but she was helping him with the trees. He had invited her to spend Christmas with him and his daughter but Theo had declined. It was essential to become accustomed to her own company again. She loved her cottage, her job and her life. Cat was good company, and like a hot water bottle most nights. The last thing she needed was a man. Her track record was abysmal.

'Where have you gone?' Tim nudged her.

'To places I shouldn't.' The rows of Christmas trees around her were not the plane trees of a Parisian boulevard in June.

'Excellent, I like the sound of that.' He grinned.

'No, I was thinking what a mess I made of my life, with Piers.'

'The man with the piercing Daniel Craig eyes rattled you.' He pointed to another tree. 'Entrance hall for Toby?'

7

She agreed and handed him a ribbon. The tree stood a good fifteen feet tall. Toby had regaled her with tales of his mother Lady Alice's love of Christmas. For Lady Alice, Theo's great-grandmother, the bigger the tree the better. According to Toby, Lady Alice had made the holiday magical. Well, it would appear that Theo had inherited that from Lady Alice, along with her looks. It continued to unsettle her to see pictures of her great-grandmother, whom she had known nothing of before she had bought Boatman's cottage two years ago. Theo's world had opened up after she'd moved in and found the hidden letters written from the First World War battlefields of France. It had led her to family she didn't know she had, like her great-uncle Toby, her cousin Jeanette and her great-grandmother Lady Alice.

Theo couldn't blame her paternal grandmother, Claire, from hiding the fact that she had never married Lady Alice's son John. In the 1940s that was a shameful thing. Claire was engaged to John when he was shot down over the Channel in the Second World War. Claire had done everything to protect the child she was carrying, and she'd held onto the love she had shared with him. That had been enough to sustain her over her long and happy life. She never sought another love in all those years. Claire was enough in herself. Theo's great-grandmother, Lady Alice, was only fifty-four when her second husband died and she continued to thrive alone. That was what Theo was now doing; thriving.

'There's another tree over there that will be perfect for Jeanette,' said Tim.

Theo refocused on the task at hand. 'Maybe a bit too wide.'

'Do you think so?' He tilted his head to one side.

She stepped up to the tree and took out her tape measure.

'You know your phone will do that,' Tim tutted.

'It may, but I'm old school.' She adjusted the Santa hat feeling more 'old fool' than 'old school'.

'I always thought you could teach old dogs new tricks.'

'Ouch!' Theo handed him the end of the tape measure. As she had guessed it was just too wide for Jeanette's sitting room.

'So why don't you want to find love again?' Tim walked towards another tree.

Theo let the tape measure snap back. 'Because I don't.'

Tim pulled in his chin. 'Is that what you said to David when he asked too many questions?'

'Hmm . . . might have.' She shrugged, feeling seen.

'Tell me all. How did you marry such an awful man?'

She wasn't sure whether to answer it or not. 'I was engaged to Piers but filled with doubts.' She tugged on a branch of a Norman Fir. It had great needle retention but no scent. She wrinkled her nose. 'Before the wedding when I was in Paris writing my dissertation I met an artist, Patrick, and did the unthinkable, the unforgivable really . . . '

Tim's eyes opened wide, and she braced herself for his comment, but before he could respond his phone rang.

'Sorry, I have to take this.' He wandered off and Theo let her mind head back to Paris in 1986.

Theo entered the bistro with her new friend, Patrick. He was welcomed by the woman behind the bar who called him Patreek. He pointed to a table on the pavement and Theo took a seat while he held a conversation with the woman in fast French that she couldn't follow.

Theo ran her hand over the red and white checked tablecloth to steady her nerves. From the kitchens, the aroma of garlic and onion mixed in the early evening air with the Gauloises cigarette smoke from a man standing nearby in the shade of a kiosk. The street was quiet, with an older couple sat at the only other outside table.

Patrick returned, holding a bottle of wine and two glasses.

'I thought I was buying you a drink?'

He grinned and she had the feeling that was how he got his own way all the time, and boy it worked. 'Maybe at the next place.' He sat beside her.

'The next place?'

'Mais oui.' His French was flawless as he raised his hand in a Gallic gesture. Laughter bubbled in her. 'So, what brings you to Paris?'

What brought Theo to Paris? Her dissertation, or more truthfully her fear, but what could she say?

'Wrong question?' He tilted his head. 'Not the museums, the architecture, the strange artists . . . ' His voice trailed away when a woman brought bread and olives to the table.

'But of course, the gardens.' He tapped her notebook which poked out of her rucksack.

Theo's left hand was bare. Her mother said she would be mugged with a three carat diamond ring on her finger. Her mother continued that if Theo was going to do this stupid thing and go to Paris for a month alone, she would look after it while Theo was away. Patrick had no way of knowing that he was flirting with a woman who wasn't free, unless Theo told him.

'I came to Paris.' Theo paused, 'to finish my dissertation and for inspiration.'

'And have you found any?' He poured the wine then he looked at her from under his long dark lashes.

Her heart raced. This was reckless. She never did reckless. But . . .

'Maybe.' She lifted the wine to her mouth and tasted the sharp sweetness of the cold rosé. Was that what he would taste like if she kissed him?

'Good.' He raised his glass to her. 'Here's to inspiration.'

Her glance met his. It was five o'clock. The sun was still hot and the air still. Both Theo and Paris were breathless.

Tim wandered back and tapped her arm. 'You were saying. You fell for a dishy artist in Paris even though your fiancé was back home?' He studied her with half-closed eyes. 'You *are* a dark horse.'

'And you are filled with clichés!' She tied a pink ribbon on another tree and ticked off the one for the library at Abbotswood.

'And David is Patrick's child?'

'Yes, but I only found this out for certain a few years ago.' She drew a breath. There was nothing she could change about the past but there were moments when she wished she would be given the chance. 'I tried to call the wedding off, but before I could, Piers admitted his affair with his father's secretary and I went ahead knowing I was no better than he.'

'I see.' Tim narrowed his glance.

'I'm not sure you do.' Could anyone? No, only two people knew the truth and they had both lived with it. 'But after years of marriage to Piers, watching his continuous infidelity, I escaped only when his secretary was pregnant with his child, or someone's child.'

'Oh.' Tim took a step back, his mouth gaping.

'Close your mouth.' She laughed. 'I am done with love.'

'My darling Theo, you are now ready for it. You're finally you and you're finally OK with yourself. Love will find you because you love yourself.'

'That's profound.' She circled an item on the list. Did she know herself now? That was something she hadn't spent any time thinking about in a long while. But she did love herself and she couldn't have said that just after the divorce.

'Wish I could take credit for it, but it was my grandmother who said that.' He rolled his eyes. 'She said that I chose Kelvin because I didn't believe I was good enough.'

'Oh Tim. You are perfection.'

'Well I think the same of you,' he said.

'Let's form a mutual admiration society, shall we?' Theo asked, her heart full of love for Tim.

The man with the Daniel Craig blue eyes, as Tim had described him, stopped at a nearby tree and caught her glance. Theo immediately opened her notebook and focused on all the trees they needed.

'He has nice cheekbones too and that's a pretty awesome smile.' Tim nudged her.

'Fine, you ask him for a date.'

He looked from Theo to the man in question. 'You know I might, but I have the distinct impression he's not interested in a toy boy, but you.'

'Enough. Let's get this job done.' She walked straight to the perfect tree for the sitting room at Abbotswood, recalling the first time she had had the privilege of dressing the hotel for Christmas. It had also been for David and Natasha's wedding. She was so blessed.

Chapter Two

Theo stood at the reception desk of Abbotswood Hotel and adjusted the small arrangement of holly and dried hydrangea heads. The balance was wrong. Pulling one flower head out she moved it to the other side, which was better but still wasn't right. Maybe she should begin again. She dropped her hands to her side and stepped back. It worked but it wasn't her best by far. She was in a hypercritical mood.

It was the first of December and this week many hands were needed to make the garlands for the hotel and several of the houses she was decorating. Tim was currently chatting to Gayle, Abbotswood's head gardener, about the foliage that they required from the estate. There were also four wreath-making workshops beginning this Friday. Theo enjoyed these moments of teaching, watching people's creativity flourish as they warmed to their task. Sadly the classes weren't yet sold out. Many people were still cautious of groups after the pandemic. The kitchen staff, however, were pressing for numbers for the lunch that was included with the workshops.

'Theo, we've had six new bookings,' the receptionist said.

'Excellent.' Theo updated her notebook.

'Which only leaves two open spaces on each of the workshops.'

'I'll do another social media push and see if we can fill them.' She made a note to update her Instagram account.

'And intriguingly,' the receptionist said, 'We've had one man book onto all four workshops.'

'One man?' Theo looked up from her notebook.

'Yes, an Erik Andersson.'

'Scandi?'

'I think so, lovely voice.' Her expression softened with a faraway look.

Theo shook her head. It had been a long time since she had reacted like that to a man's voice.

'So, he called?' Most bookings were completed online. The world had changed so much. Gone were telephone calls and posting letters. They seemed old-fashioned now. Did one hold onto a love note that was sent via text or email? Did they have the same meaning? Those letters from the First World War she had found in her cottage were so poignant. Her ex-husband had never written more than a birthday card to her. She had written to him while she had been away in Paris, but her heart hadn't been in it.

'Yes, he'd heard all about you,' she said.

Theo stepped back from the desk. 'Not sure I like the sound of that.'

'He didn't seem threatening at all . . . just keen.'

'Hmm, fair enough.' Theo picked up her notebook. 'Anything else?'

'Yes, this weekend we also have a twentieth wedding anniversary being celebrated and they have asked for special flowers.' She handed Theo an email. It stated that this was a surprise, and these were the flowers in his wife's wedding bouquet, and if possible, he'd love an arrangement made with them. Theo adored tasks like this. Since her divorce she had loved nothing more than helping other people have happy weddings and anniversaries.

The receptionist took a call and Theo went into the wood-panelled front hall where the fire blazed, warming the cold day. The circular table in the centre was bare, waiting for her to bring in the new flower arrangement. On Sunday, Advent began in earnest as her brother Martin had reminded her while picking her brain on the topic of his sermon. He too had asked her to spend Christmas with him in Oxford, along with the other Jesuits he lived with. But she didn't want to spend Christmas with a bunch of priests, as much fun as they were. No, this year she would spend it quietly and reflect on how blessed she was. It would be simply her, Cat and silence.

'I brought this over for you.' Tim placed the arrangement down on the table and he adjusted the branches. His sense of design was superb. He had been wasted in the City. But if he hadn't been there with a high paying job, he wouldn't have been able to walk out after his partner so publicly dumped and humiliated him. Tim wouldn't discuss it but when his mother, Francis, had visited she had told Theo all she knew. Francis had been so pleased when Tim had packed the city in and left the bastard behind.

'Gayle has brought in a ton of greenery.' He plucked a piece out of his hair and twirled it in the space between them. 'Can you have a look and tell her what else you need?'

Theo nodded but remained distracted as she walked towards the tree which was undecorated. Where possible she gave them a day or two to settle before she trimmed them. But today the lights would go on. This was a job she loved and loathed in equal measure. Hopefully the lights had been stored well and she would discover the strands she had carefully wound together last January weren't tangled or half dead. In the evenings she and Cat had been working with wire and twigs to make small reindeer ornaments for these trees.

The ones for her cousin Jeanette's house were sprayed with non-environmentally friendly purple and silver metallic paint. The finished effect looked amazing and if she repurposed them next year the use of the paint wouldn't be so awful. Theo had tried to dissuade Jeannette, but she was determined to have a silver and purple Christmas. Jeanette was entertaining a new man, Louis, and he had silver hair that matched the ornaments. Theo was only surprised that Jeanette hadn't talked the poor man into dying it purple. The retired barrister was a steadying influence on the volatile Jeanette who had been seeing him for four months. There had been no signs Jeanette was pushing him out of the door, surprising everyone including Jeanette herself.

The tree in the hotel's sitting room had settled well but it was further from a fireplace and happier for it. Today if all went well they would complete the garland for the main door and for the fire-surrounds. Christmas would fully happen after the past few years of pandemic when things were so different. If she let her thoughts go back to 2018, when she was married and had a huge house, she could see now how unhappy she was back then. As her mother, Virginia, had repeatedly said to Theo over the years, she had made her bed and she must lie in it. Theo had done so for far too long.

Virginia was also on her own this Christmas but spending it with her would make Christmas more like hell than heaven. Theo had loved this holiday for as long as she could remember. It had been her father's and her grandmother's favourite time of year. As a vicar her father had reminded his congregation every Christmas that it was a time of goodwill and a time to treat others with respect. This, he would add, included the other shoppers in the stores when it came to acquiring the last double cream left on the shelves. Nowadays that rush to have everything and then some in the house was unnecessary. Stores were open on Boxing Day unlike the not-so-distant past. Despite that certainty though, Theo intended to have enough food in so that she didn't have to move for four days.

On that fourth day she would need to check the flowers at the hotel and begin gathering everything for Gayle and Hugo's wedding. This one, like David's, had to be perfect. Gayle and Hugo, the manager of Abbotswood, had been her first friends in her new life here. Her brother, Martin, was presiding over the marriage and Theo was tasked with making the hotel special for both of them using what was available in January. Sustainability was high on both Gayle's and Hugo's agenda. Fortunately, the garden was sheltered and already blooms would be appearing. Gayle had agreed that early white Sol daffodils from Cornwall were allowed. These small white blooms were so heavenly scented and spoke so much of hope and the coming spring that Theo adored them and used them as much as she could.

Hugo walked into the sitting room, grinning. 'It's beginning to look a lot like Christmas.'

'Just.' Theo assessed her handiwork.

'Why don't you join Gayle and I here for Christmas lunch?'

She laughed. 'I'm getting the impression you're all worried about me. I'm happy to be on my own. I could have accepted the invite from David, Martin, Tim or Toby.'

Hugo held out his hands in front of him like a barrister pleading a case. 'We'd love your company.'

'Thanks.' She adjusted a branch in an arrangement by the fireplace. 'I appreciate it but I'm looking forward to a quiet few days. It's been hectic of late.'

'It has, with David's move and you helping with their house. Please know you are welcome even at the last minute if you change your mind.'

'I appreciate that.' Theo touched his arm. 'Now I must get the garlands going.'

'Tim already has it underway.'

'Gosh, if I'm not careful he'll have my job!' She stepped back.

Hugo tilted his head and said, 'Only if you wanted him to.'

Theo watched him disappear into the dining room, thinking that was an odd comment. Why on earth would she want to give up the job that she loved?

Chapter Three

The cobbled stable yard smelled of Christmas with so many types of cedar, pine and fir ready for the workshop. Theo had yet to make the wreaths for the doors here at Abbotswood and she might be able to finish one during the workshop depending on how capable the participants were.

She paused on the threshold, surveying the long room filled with a large table covered in a white oilcloth. Tim had laid out the copper frames for the wreaths on each of the twelve places.

'Bublé or Bing?' Tim asked. 'Or more radical, like Billy Idol?'

'Didn't he only do one Christmas song?' She straightened the copper frame in front of her.

'No, he did a whole album.'

She looked up from the table and studied him. 'I've only heard "Jingle Bell Rock".'

He shrugged. 'What about Jamie Cullum's Christmas album?'

Theo placed a roll of wire on each place. 'A mix of Bing and Bublé will do nicely.'

'Yes, ma'am.' He saluted and soon the dulcet tones of Bing Crosby filled the room. Theo hummed along with her thoughts drifting back to her childhood again. 'Can you put on the one Bing did with Bowie?'

'Feeling nostalgic?' he asked.

'Yes, and just wishing they had done more than one.'

'Me too.'

Theo sang loudly while she pulled her baskets of ribbons and sprayed pine cones out from under a side table. A deep baritone joined in, and she sat up suddenly, banging her head on the underside of the table.

'Sorry, did I startle you?' The voice was rich and accented.

Theo nodded with her eyes shut. This must be the man who had booked the four classes. Now she understood the receptionist's expression.

'It's my favourite and I can't help singing along.'

Theo sat back on her knees while rubbing her head and stared. It was the man with the blue, blue eyes.

'Let me help.' He picked up the basket. 'On the big table or just here?'

Behind him Tim swooned, or pretended to, and Theo put her hand over her mouth to hide her smile.

'Right there,' she pointed to the table beside her, 'is good.'

He placed the basket down and held out a hand to help her up.

Theo hesitated then berated herself. What was she afraid of? A man who signed up for wreath making classes? She took his hand and stood. The connection was instant, and startled by it she looked up from their hands. The blue, blue eyes danced with mischief and without saying a word told her he felt it too.

'I'm Erik,' he said, still holding her hand.

'I'm Theo,' she said despite her dry mouth. The last time someone's touch made her feel this way had been in Paris over thirty years ago. Surely that couldn't happen again.

'Hi Erik, glad you made it.' Tim grinned like he was crazy,

crazy happy with an *I told you so expression* covering his handsome face.

Theo took her hand back and worked on her breathing. It took a few moments to return to normal.

'Nice to see you again.' Erik looked from Theo to Tim.

Tim hadn't said a word when she mentioned there was a man taking all four workshops. She was about to haul him out of the room for a chat when five women who took the course every year arrived, and from that moment on she couldn't find a minute alone with Tim out of earshot of everyone else.

'As you will see when we head to the courtyard, Gayle has done us proud with this fabulous array of greenery.' Theo picked up a branch that she had selected earlier. 'When you're choosing remember many times the underside of the foliage is as lovely as the front and will add interesting colour and texture to your wreath.' With the branch of cypress, she showed the silvery underside. The participants headed out and she lingered, hoping to grab Tim but he had dashed for the door, avoiding her like a naughty child.

She joined the others in the courtyard where her breath made clouds in the crisp air. The Christmas music began to work its magic on her. Theo couldn't be cross with him.

Two women needed her help to trim some of the branches so it was a while until she could pull Tim aside.

'You knew?'

He tried to keep a straight face. 'When you nipped into the loo at the tree farm I spoke to him and he explained that he was trying to decorate his son's house for him.'

Theo frowned.

'His son lost his husband to cancer two Christmases ago and he had been doing nothing but work trying to avoid his grief.'

'Oh, poor man.' Theo watched Erik carefully examine the variety of the cypress branches. 'Why take the course four times?'

'Needs more than four wreaths but it is a start and he figures he will understand the process by then.' Tim bent to pick up a pine cone. 'And I think he liked the look of the instructor.'

'You, you mean.' She sent him a sideways glance.

'Honey, it's not me.' He laughed and helped one of the women untangle some holly branches.

Theo followed the women back inside. She had made a selection of greenery earlier, ready to demonstrate the process of constructing a wreath to the desired size. Once everyone had returned she noticed that Erik was still lingering about the greenery looking a bit daunted. She picked up her secateurs and walked back out into the bright cold morning.

'Can I help?' She came to his side.

He straightened to his full height. 'Am I holding the demonstration back?'

Theo thought about lying but decided against it. 'A bit.'

'I was looking for straw.'

Theo tilted her head. 'I expected many things but not straw.'

'In Sweden our wreaths have an inner circle of straw.'

'I'm afraid we don't have any on-hand today, but I may be able to source some for tomorrow and certainly for next weekend's workshops.' She would also have to do a search on Swedish Christmas wreaths. Something itched at the back of her mind, but she couldn't place it.

'I will make an English one today.' He collected his array of greenery and followed her inside where he took his place in the middle of the table. They all gathered around as she began to show how to secure the sphagnum moss to the frame to provide a firm base and moisture for the greenery.

'This moss,' Theo held a clump up, 'is legally sourced from Holland but is protected here in the UK so don't collect it from the wild!' She looked at them all. 'It attracts moisture so it will keep the wreaths fresh for the whole holiday season.'

She explained the need to secure the moss tightly with the copper wire then went around to inspect everyone's progress while Tim assisted with the arrival of coffee and tea. Most seemed to catch on quickly, but Erik's moss was not evenly or securely attached. Theo held out her hand and unwound what he'd done so far. 'You need to keep it the same thickness and tight. This is the base that will keep the whole wreath stable.'

He watched her closely.

'How big a wreath do you need?' She took another handful of moss.

'A big one so I think the frame is too small.' His face was intent as he waved his hand in a circle.

'This frame will make a big wreath but you will need a thicker padding of moss.' She handed him the frame after she had added and secured two handfuls of moss. 'Now you try.'

'My wife had been very good at this sort of thing but I am hopeless.'

She stopped and met his glance. 'Have you ever tried before?'

'No.'

'Then you don't know if you are awful.'

'True.' He smiled and the creases beside his eyes deepened making him all the more attractive. She didn't want to feel attraction so moved on to help another participant.

After the moss was secure for everyone, she encouraged them to grab a drink and a biscuit. Once they had settled again, she began to show how to cut the ends of the branches to fit into the moss.

'Also think about the length of the pieces and where the wreath will hang.' She held up a frame and placed a long piece on it to reveal how big the ensuing wreath would be.

Erik looked at her intently then to the mass of branches piled in front of him. His confusion was clear and she looked to see if Tim could assist, but he was sandwiched between two of the older women, helping them. Theo walked over to Erik.

'I don't know where to start.' He held up his hands.

'As we begin at the outside of the wreath, you want to choose a branch that is strong and sets the size of the wreath you need.'

He rummaged through the pile and pulled out a big branch of Douglas fir.

'Good choice. Now cut the end at an angle so it will fit into the moss.'

She took the branch from him and noted the hints of red paint around his cuticles. Once she slipped the fir into the moss she wrapped the wire around both it and the frame. 'Now choose another one that appeals to you that's a bit different.'

He picked up a yew and flipped it to the silvery side.

'Nice,' she said. 'Remember to cut it on the right angle.'

He cut it correctly and handed it to her. She secured it in on the inside of the fir then wrapped the wire around both. Running her fingers over the branches, she said, 'Now can you see how the wreath will be this big?' She made a circle around the frame. 'Will that be big enough?'

He frowned but then nodded. 'This will work.'

'Good.' She spread his selection of branches a bit further apart on the table. 'Now choose another piece of foliage and I will watch you do it.'

He took a piece of variegated ivy and secured it, followed by another fir piece.

She grinned. 'Good, you're on track now.'

'Thank you,' he said. With one last glance at him, she walked away surveying the focused faces on all the attendees.

Everyone worked happily to complete the green part of the wreath. As a few were ready, she performed a quick demonstration with the one she had made earlier on how to add embellishments. She wired in a few pheasant feathers and some pine cones before demonstrating a simple way to construct a bow from some raffia.

The students rummaged through the baskets of ribbons, feathers, pine cones and ornaments. This was where their personalities really appeared with their choice of coloured ribbon and if they chose to spray with fake snow or use only natural adornments. Each wreath was unique, which she loved. Occasionally she jumped in to correct one she could see going wrong, but mostly she was in awe of the change in the participants as they created something beautiful.

'It smells like Christmas in here,' Hugo said as he came to check on the timing for lunch. Soon they would finish their wreaths, clear the table, and lunch would be served in here while the music added another festive layer to the proceedings. All was as it should be, except for Erik. Emergency help was required.

'I'll take charge of the clean-up,' said Tim. 'That needs your help.' He pointed to Erik's lopsided wreath. The array of foliage was beautiful but it looked like there had been a car crash on one side. Theo held it up and looked at the imbalance. It could be fixed but she had never seen a wreath go quite this wrong. Before she did anything she asked Erik, 'Was this your plan?'

He nodded.

'And you're pleased with it?'

He shrugged.

'What exactly were you trying to do?'

'I was trying to do them like my wife used to,' he said. 'She would take a circular frame and cover half of it.'

'I see.'

'I didn't pay enough attention and now it is too long since . . .' his voice trailed away.

'She's no longer with you,' Theo whispered.

He cleared his throat. 'She died twenty years ago.'

'I'm sorry.' Those words never said enough but she had

never found any others that could begin to say what she wanted to say.

He looked up from his wreath. 'I need to move on from the Christmases she created and try something new.'

'Or you could blend the new and the treasured.' Theo smiled. 'I suggest this wreath becomes a traditional British one as the moss goes all the way around and it would look a bit odd without the branches.

'Agreed.' He stepped back and shoved his hands in his pockets.

'I'm not going to fix it, you are,' she said beckoning him closer. 'Select some more branches first in varying sizes.' She unwound the wire back to the point where the density changed and handed it to Erik. It was obvious that he wanted her to fix it, and she could, but that was not the point of the workshop, and he was doing three more.

He began at the outside edge as she had taught him and began working his way around. She liked his use of the varying foliage and soon the wreath began to take proper shape.

'Well done.' She shifted through some of the foliage and sorted them into the different sizes so he could work swiftly. One of the ladies brought over some of her greenery and before long Erik's wreath was finished and the waiters could lay the table.

'That looks wonderful and it's huge. You can decorate it after lunch if that's OK.' He studied her and she lifted a hand to push her hair back self-conscious of her workmanlike appearance, and she probably had pine needles in her hair.

'Hello,' a very familiar gravely voice said. 'What have we here?'

The ever elegant, Jeanette walked from behind Theo and held out her hand to Erik. 'I'm Jeanette Neville, and you are?'

'Erik Andersson. Hello.'

'I might start attending these things if men as dishy as Erik are going to be taking part.' Jeanette chuckled in that deeply dirty way of hers. She oozed pure feminine charm as she admired his wreath and Theo felt a stab of jealousy, something that hadn't troubled her for some time. Mostly she was jealous of her cousin's ease with herself and the world as a whole. Of course she wasn't jealous because of Erik Andersson.

'I just popped in to say that I loved the wire reindeer and to confirm I'll see you on Sunday? I'm desperate for the tree to go up on the first Sunday of advent.'

Erik turned to Theo. 'You work on Sundays?'

'Frequently, as events take place on Sunday and I have several houses as well as the hotel to decorate in time for Christmas.'

'You decorate people's houses?' He looked from Theo to Jeanette.

'She does a divine job of it and I can simply enjoy the beauty without the hassle.' Jeanette grinned. 'And Sunday is my day!' She looked at Theo who nodded. 'Father Christmas, eat your heart out.'

He looked a bit puzzled. His English was impeccable but maybe that phrase didn't translate.

'Jeanette meant that Santa would be jealous, but I'm not sure that purple and silver are his colours.'

'Of course they are,' said Tim coming to join them. 'Hugo is looking for you Jeanette, he said something about Christmas lunch.'

Jeanette grinned. 'Yes, we decided to come here for the big day and let someone else do the cooking. You will join us, won't you Theo?' She fixed Theo with a hard stare.

'Thank you but no. It's a quiet Christmas for me and Cat, and I'm looking forward to it.'

Jeanette pouted but disappeared out the door without another word.

'How lovely . . . you will spend Christmas with your partner,' Erik said.

Theo turned to him keeping a straight face. 'Cat is my Norwegian Forest cat.'

'Oh.' The creases around his eyes deepened with his smile and Theo's stomach tightened a bit. She couldn't deny how attractive he was. 'So you will spend Christmas alone,' he continued.

'Yes, and I'm looking forward to it, but everyone seems to think I'm lying and I'm not.'

'Me thinks you protest too much,' said Tim, pushing a broom past and allowing Erik's place to be laid at the table.

Theo swung around ready to hit him but he had scooted off.

'Erik, take a seat. Your lunch will be arriving in a moment.'

Theo spoke to another attendee then sat at the head of the table to enjoy the food. But her glance kept meeting Erik's and she couldn't have said what she had actually eaten.

Chapter Four

With Jeanette's Christmas trees in a trailer, Theo set off early. The plan included Theo spending the night so they could have dinner and wine after the decoration was finished. They hadn't had a good catch-up in a while and she looked forward to it. Cat, however, was not pleased. Once the timed food bowl went down, Cat knew that she wouldn't see Theo again tonight and the feline had sent her the most dismissive look as she had left.

Jeanette lived half an hour away in a beautiful modern house with large windows that framed the glorious views across the countryside. It suited Jeanette to a tee. There was no fuss, and aside from a few paintings, Jeanette was the oldest thing in it as she neared eighty. Not that she looked or acted her age. In fact she had a younger and freer outlook than Theo.

Once down the long track that Theo called her drive, she turned on Radio Four. It was a program all about loneliness at Christmas. She sighed. She was not lonely but she was alone. That was a big difference. She shut the radio off. Yes, she missed David and his family but she didn't miss the mess, the noise and the general chaos. This was her life going forward and she was embracing it, if not looking forward to it.

The silence in the car bothered her though. The absence of

noise was good but right now she didn't want it. With a few presses of the button, classical music filled the space and her shoulders dropped down. She had begun to take things much too seriously. Everyone cared, that's why they were all inviting her. It wasn't that they didn't believe her, and with that thought she turned into the lane that climbed to Jeanette's.

In the low December light, Jeanette had already switched on the white fairy lights that covered the exterior of the house and adorned the evergreen shrubs. Theo's spirits lifted as she parked and grabbed the wreath she'd made for Jeanette from the passenger seat. It was covered in small purple glass balls, sprayed silver pine cones, and a glittery bow finished with a purple wire reindeer.

The front door opened wide and Jeanette beamed at her. 'Is that gorgeous thing for me?'

'Don't know anyone else who would want it,' Theo said.

'It's glorious!' Jeanette took it from her hands. 'Now do you want coffee or a Buck's Fizz?'

Theo laughed. 'We have trees to fit into bases let alone trim. Coffee first and maybe the drink at lunchtime?'

Jeanette sighed. 'If we must.' She lifted the wreath onto her glossy black front door.

'I have to say it's perfect.' Despite the over-the-top nature of the trimming, it worked against the sleek backdrop. Theo stepped back, pleased with her work.

Jeanette shimmied a bit. 'I knew it would and I've sourced some more ornaments for the trees and found the most divine purple candles.'

'Never have I decorated for Christmas in the colour of lent.'

'It's good to shake things up.'

Theo followed Jeanette to the kitchen. The back wall was all window overlooking the enclosed infinity lap pool, and the view never ceased to take Theo's breath away even on a dull day like today. Jeanette swam daily so it was practical and not simply for appearances. In a clever design trick the pool's glass walls could be retracted in fine weather. If Theo wanted a swim, the Tamar was on her doorstep, however the water temperature was a bit more refreshing than Jeanette's solar heated pool.

Jeanette handed her a mug filled with strong Italian coffee. 'Where do we start?'

Theo cradled the mug in her hands. 'Bringing the trees into the house while we're feeling strong.'

'Fine.'

'Then the lights.' Theo ran through the list in her head.

'Then lunch?' Jeanette pulled a quiche out of the oven.

'Definitely.' Theo sniffed the air. Jeanette was a superb cook. She'd explained it was because of her years in France, but Theo knew exposure to good food did not make one a cook. That took skill and instinct. Theo managed quite well but she didn't have Jeanette's flare or lightness of touch.

Once Theo had finished her coffee, she headed to the trailer. The sooner the trees were in and up, the sooner she could dive into that quiche. Jeanette followed with gardening gloves in hand. Theo didn't bother. Her hands were toughened by the continuous work with flowers. Only when pruning roses and clearing weeds did she bother. However Jeanette's hands were beautifully manicured and it would be a shame to chip the glossy black nail varnish she wore.

Theo took the heavy end of the largest tree out and Jeanette grabbed the top. Together they propped it by the front door. The remaining two trees Theo could manage on her own. Jeanette took the bases for them from the car.

'Do you want to place those where you want the trees?' Theo asked.

'No, we discussed it, and you know where they are going. I'm going to pop into the greenhouse and harvest some salad to go with the lunch.'

Theo shrugged and located the largest base for the sitting room. It would be easier getting this tree upright if she had Jeanette's help. But she knew better than to try and convince Jeanette to do something she didn't want to.

Theo placed the empty base four foot from the glass wall. The floor was sealed slate and didn't need protection from any overflowing water or dropping needles. No matter how good or freshly cut the tree, there would be some needle drop by the sixth of January.

Outside again, Theo tilted the tree towards her shoulder. It was seven foot tall and not the easiest thing to manoeuvre through the front door.

'Can I give you a hand?'

Theo turned, recognising the slightly accented English. What on earth was Erik Andersson doing at Jeanette's?

'Yes, thank you,' she said, trying to hide the surprise she felt.

He took the bottom of the tree and Theo led the way into the sitting room with her head full of questions. By the base she stopped and without asking any further instruction Erik lowered his end into the holder while she held the tree straight. He adjusted the bolts.

'Do you want to check if it's upright? I'll make sure it doesn't fall.'

Theo nodded, distracted by his presence. Once she was a good six feet from him and the tree she could think. Jeanette must have invited him but why? That woman never did anything without a purpose. He was very attractive so maybe he would be, or possibly already was, her next conquest.

'That looks great.' She walked back to hold the tree while he tightened the bolts securely. Once he was done, she went to her car for the watering can. The dull day had turned into a mizzly one. She filled the can from the garden tap and walked back into the sitting room. Erik had disappeared and she breathed a sigh of relief. Once the base was filled, she took off the twine that

32

held the branches tight to the trunk. She loved this moment when the tree relaxed. Ideally she would do no more today and let the tree become used to the warmth of the environment. Sadly her schedule didn't allow for that. Tomorrow and Tuesday she would finish the hotel, Wednesday was set for the charity Christmas tree competition in the local church. Thursday it was meeting with potential clients for three spring weddings. Friday and Saturday were wreath workshops, and Sunday was decorating with Toby. A daunting week but all fun.

She placed the next base in the kitchen, then went to retrieve the tree from the trailer. Erik appeared around the side of the house. 'I was admiring the greenhouse. Sorry I wasn't here to help.'

'Not a problem, I can carry this one myself.'

'True, but it is always easier with two.' He lifted the trunk to prove his point. Theo balanced the top on her shoulder and headed to the kitchen. Jeanette was mixing salad dressing when they walked in.

'Erik will be joining us.'

'Great,' Theo said, not thinking great but wondering why. This was a day for Jeanette and her to catch up, not to have an unknown third party in their midst.

'Erik's son's house is remote and he doesn't know anyone in the area.' She smiled at them both like a benign queen but Theo knew better.

Theo stood on a ladder and held the tree from the top while Erik twisted the tree in the base until it was less like the Leaning Tower of Pisa. This was the narrow tree Theo and Tim had selected so that it would be easier to get around it.

'He's trying to finish the decorating for his son.'

Theo looked down and straight into Erik's eyes. He grinned and she glanced away.

'He has convinced his son to spend at least one Christmas there as it was a house his son had bought with his husband. It

33

was a project that Peter, Oskar's husband, was doing when he was diagnosed with an inoperable brain tumour.'

Erik tightened the bolts in the base. Theo looked from him to Jeanette and back again. Jeanette had acquired a lot of information about Erik and his son.

'Yes, Oskar intends to sell the house.' Erik shrugged. 'I don't think he should, or at least not yet.'

Intrigued Theo asked, 'Why?'

'He's avoiding his grief.' He pulled a small branch from his hair. 'I know this because I did the same for twenty years and missed out on life by working and doing little else.'

'And you don't want your son to do the same.' Theo understood. No parent wanted their child to suffer, and especially not to repeat one's own mistakes.

'No, I don't.' He sighed. 'But sadly this is what I taught him to do. By finishing the house I hope to wake him up and encourage him to grieve.'

Jeanette handed him a glass of champagne. Theo glanced at the clock. It was one. Where had the time gone? Jeanette gave her a glass too.

'Here's to new friends and happy Christmases.' Jeanette raised her glass.

Erik looked at Jeanette then directly into Theo's eyes and said, 'Skål!'

'Cheers.' Theo glanced from Jeanette to Erik, trying to read the dynamic. She sensed nothing. Possibly Jeanette was simply being neighbourly but somehow Theo doubted it. Jeanette, whether she said so or not, did everything with a purpose, her own unique purpose.

Theo put her glass down and went to collect the watering can before she lost track of what she needed to do. There was another tree to install in Jeanette's bedroom, then at least the trees were all in situ. Rather than interrupt Jeanette and Erik in the kitchen, she detoured to position the base. This room, like the kitchen, had a glass wall facing the view and another of the walls consisted of floor to ceiling books. Above the large bed was a portrait of Jeanette nude. She was lying on her stomach looking back over her shoulder at the viewer. It was mischievous and provocative at the same time. The artist had captured the essence of her that still existed even though Jeanette had mentioned the painting had been done forty years ago.

Erik entered with the tree. This one was smaller and quite easy to manage. He set it in the stand and Theo held it while he secured it. Once he filled the base, she freed the tree from the twine.

'Lunch is ready,' Jeanette called from the kitchen.

Theo cleared up the twine while Erik went ahead, and then joined them in the kitchen. The large table was laid for three and the champagne was in an ice bucket. Jeanette brought the quiche to the table and Erik the salad. Theo gathered the bread and the bowl of small potatoes before sitting down.

Jeanette turned on some Christmas music and topped up everyone's glass. 'This works out well as I've told Erik that he can stay tonight too and not have to worry about driving.'

Theo nearly choked on her champagne. There was only one guest bedroom. What should she do?

'I was telling Erik about the stunning renovation you had done on Boatman's cottage.' Jeanette tossed the salad then sat.

'She said you had an incredible eye for detail and period features.' He handed her the quiche.

Theo took a piece, debating what to say. If she simply said thanks then it would kill the conversation. 'I took on a large renovation project years ago with my ex-husband. It was mostly Georgian but had both earlier and later features.'

He nodded. 'My son's property is like that. It is a farmhouse with grandeur and lots of Victorian extensions.'

'Sounds lovely.' Theo leaned in. 'Is it only the farmhouse or are there outbuildings? And what of the farm itself?'

'Many outbuildings and about ten acres of land, most of which is let to the local farmer who lives in a warm newly-built house.'

'That is the problem with old houses, especially now. You need to earn a fortune to heat them.' Jeanette looked around her kitchen pleased. Her house was well insulated and had solar panels on the south facing roof, and a heat pump as well.

'Where do you live Erik?' Theo asked.

'I have an apartment in Stockholm but until last year I lived in the Far East, working.'

'You've retired?' Jeanette opened a bottle of white wine.

'Yes, they were downsizing and offered me early retirement, and,' he paused, 'it was time to return.'

'You didn't want to?' Theo put her hand over the glass. Until she knew what the sleeping arrangements were she wasn't having any more.

'When Oskar lost Peter and threw himself into his work to the exclusion of all else, I saw the error of my own ways. I'm fifty-nine and I hope I have a chance to enjoy life and maybe love again.' He glanced Theo's way and she quickly gulped the last of her champagne.

'Excellent news. I do believe in embracing life and love.' Jeanette clapped her hands. 'I have enjoyed so much of both.'

'It shows in your beauty.' Erik said as he took a piece of bread. 'What are the decoration plans?'

'Theo has it all organised. I believe the next step is the lights. At this time of year you can never have enough light.'

'This is true,' he said.

Jeanette darted out into pantry and Theo followed.

'What on earth are you up to?' Theo whispered.

Jeanette held up a plate of cheese. 'This.'

'No, not the cheese. You only have one guest room.'

'Oh, that.' Jeanette grinned. 'Thought you two could share as Louis is coming around later.'

Theo drew a deep breath.

'Relax. The sofa in the study pulls out into a bed.' Jeanette headed back into the kitchen while Theo stood listening to her wicked laugh. She would make it through this somehow. The problem was Erik was far too distracting.

Chapter Five

'He'd be a good one to get back in the saddle with so to speak,' Jeanette said, walking Theo out to the car. The morning sun was bright, unlike yesterday's.

'You are relentless. I don't do love, or sex or dalliance.'

'Why ever not?' Jeanette asked.

Theo climbed into the driver's seat. 'I just don't.'

'That's not an answer . . . either to me or to yourself,' she said.

Theo closed the door but Jeanette remained there, and she was forced to wind the window down or seem rude. 'Let me phrase it another way. Love doesn't do me.'

'Bollocks. All you are saying is that you didn't trust love before and therefore got it wrong. Theo, you are only fifty-eight and have years of possible love in front of you, and if not love then fun.'

'Ha.' Theo started the engine.

'Listen, I'm seventy-nine soon to be eighty. I have never committed to one love knowing I couldn't stick it out but I never shut the door on love. I have gained so much, even from the disasters.'

Theo looked at her friend shivering in the cold in an impossibly elegant négligée that belonged in another era, another place, and yet here she was pleading with Theo on this frosty morning to consider an affair of, if not the heart, at least the body.

'Think about it. Erik would be fun.'

'How do you know that?'

'You can tell these things from his laugh to the way he made omelettes for us last night while we decorated.'

'And sang drunkenly.' Theo rubbed her hands together. It was cold.

'It was such fun and the house looks glorious.'

'It does.' Erik had left before Theo had woken. 'You did hear that Erik made it back?'

Jeanette's eyes twinkled. 'I had a text.'

'Good, now before you freeze to death I need to be at work,' Theo said.

'You win for now.' Jeanette blew her a kiss then scampered into the house like a child, not a soon-to-be octogenarian. Her birthday was in February, and they were planning a surprise party for her. As Theo reversed down the drive, she thought about the logistical problems they were facing. Jeanette knew everyone, and exactly who should be included in this bash was tricky. Jeanette's twin Sophie wasn't much help as she simply kept adding to the list even though she was having a separate party of her own.

Once out on the main road, Theo turned on the radio and tried to leave thoughts of last night and the sheer joy of it all behind. God they all had laughed but that might have had something to do with the second bottle of champagne while they strung the lights and hung the baubles.

Waiting at the traffic lights to cross Greystone Bridge, Theo thought of how achingly familiar this area was to her now. Just three years ago she couldn't place where Greystone Bridge was in reference to Horsebridge and the Tamar. Under the bridge the Tamar raced with the previous month's rain. The river was now a part of her, as if she had lived by its side all her life.

The light changed and she made her way across and into Devon. The road twisted up through the woodland to the open fields, past two churches and villages until finally she turned right towards Abbotswood. The hedges allowed flashes of the fields they protected, and woolly sheep clustered together against the December cold. The sky had turned a vivid blue and yesterday's muffling murk had cleared. Today she must finish the garlands and wreaths for the hotel.

With her car parked away from the guest area, she walked through the crisp air breathing deeply. Tim was already here and Gayle walked towards her with her arms full of holly still sporting berries.

'Morning,' Theo said. 'Are those for me?'

'Who else?' Gayle joined her on the way to the stables. 'When I saw them I decided they would be perfect for the sitting room.'

'And you'd be right.' Theo eyed them, thinking it might even stretch to the library if she used them judiciously.

'We were clearing the old Duke's Drive for footpaths and these were hidden in the dense growth. Not sure even the birds would have found them.'

'The hotel will look so festive with them.'

Gayle placed the branches down in the stable yard and said, 'Coffee?'

'Yes.' They both set off to the kitchen where the aroma of bacon tickled at Theo's stomach.

'Morning you two,' said one of the waiters making coffees. 'Usual?'

'Yes, please,' Theo and Gayle said in unison.

Prep work was already under way for lunch, tea and dinner this evening. The kitchen was always a hive of activity and filled with divine aromas.

'A garden tour with tea has been booked for Friday,' the cook said.

'When did that happen?' asked Gayle.

'Yesterday afternoon.'

'It's after the workshop. Do you think you can lend a hand with the tour?' Gayle asked.

'I'm sure either Tim or I can.' Theo took her coffee. 'See you later,'

Theo looked forward to today and working with her team who would be here within the hour. Christmas would truly arrive to Abbotswood today. Tim had already begun and five foot of garland was laid on the table.

'You started early.' Theo shrugged off her coat after checking Zach's rabbit was still secure in her pocket. It was becoming a bit of a talisman for her.

'Couldn't sleep so decided to arrive at seven when I knew all would be quiet and my hands would be busy enough to shut my brain off.'

'Oh God, what did you read before bed?'

'I should know better than to look at Facebook, but I did.'

Theo walked up to Tim and wrapped her arms around him. 'He didn't deserve you.'

'I know you're right but in the small hours it's damn lonely.'

Theo nodded and she thought about Cat's warm body curled up to hers. Cat was enough to keep the loneliness of the small hours at bay. She loved the quiet of her cottage when she could sit with coffee and a book and no one to interrupt asking for something.

Sue Watson from one of Theo's flower arrangement courses appeared. 'I popped into the cottage as you asked this morning and set Cat free. She was on vocal form telling me all about her mistreatment by her human.'

Theo chuckled. 'Typical. It will have to be fresh cooked prawns for dinner to redeem myself.'

'Maybe caviar by the way she was complaining.' Sue pulled on her gloves and began sorting the greenery into piles so that Tim and Theo could work more quickly. Another two volunteers from her course would arrive shortly and then they would power ahead with the construction of these garlands.

'Tim, have you met the new village shop owner?' Sue asked.

Tim looked up. 'Don't tell me. He's gay and you think we'd make a good match?'

'Yup. About ten years older than you at a guess and he's definitely single.'

'Hmmm.' Tim wound the wire securely about the branches. 'I may have to pick up a pint of milk on my way home.'

'I think you should.' Sue handed Theo a grouping of branches as Ed and his wife Tilly arrived. They were now a complete team and Theo loved this stage where they all worked so seamlessly together. Tim chose a lively playlist of Christmas hits, and they all sang badly as they spent the morning fuelled by coffee and Christmas biscuits handmade by Ed. By lunchtime they were adorning the entrance porch with the garland and hundreds of twined white fairy lights. Christmas was on its way.

They stopped briefly for sandwiches then tackled the smaller garlands for the main fireplaces in the hotel. By four Theo was dressing the tree in the entrance hall when Jeanette appeared.

'I heard from the delicious Tim that you're in trouble with Cat, so I have brought some prawns for her and the remains of the quiche for you.' She kissed Theo's cheeks. 'I've left it in the stables where it's cold enough to keep everything fresh, including a dead body.' She shivered.

'Are you hiding one?' Theo raised an eyebrow. Jeanette wore a fake fur stole over her burgundy coat, with a beautiful jewelled holly broach. Her grey hair was immaculate. Theo pushed her own hair out of her eyes and found several pine needles and a bit of glitter from the fish shaped metal ornaments.

'Heavens, why would I do that?'

'I never know with you.' Theo smiled. 'It's always the unexpected.'

'Ah, that's because I don't beat about the bush. I walk straight to what I want, unless it's love then I may wiggle a bit.'

'You are incorrigible.'

'Absolutely.' She nodded. 'Now Martin will be here shortly and I thought we could have a drink before he goes across the river with you.'

'Martin's coming?' Theo frowned. She had spoken with her brother three days ago and there had been no mention of a visit.

'Didn't he tell you?'

'No.'

'Well he's with you until Friday evening.'

The guest room wasn't made up but at least the sheets were clean. She would need to go food shopping although she had enough in the house for tonight especially with the food that Jeanette had brought today. She stepped back to look at the tree. It was finished.

'Hello,' Martin said as he walked through the front door. 'Just the two people I wanted to see.'

'You didn't say you were coming?' Theo chided as she hugged him.

'I did but maybe you had your little brother filter on.' He kissed her cheek.

'Hmm.'

'Is it a problem? You have other guests?' He raised an eyebrow.

'No, but the bed's not made.'

'I can make a bed.'

'I know.' It didn't seem that long ago that he couldn't, or maybe wouldn't, but she wouldn't say that.

'But you, dear sis, like to have everything just right and welcoming.'

She playfully punched his armed.

'Right that's my sign to take Jeanette into the library and order a drink. What can I get you?' he asked.

'A sparkling water, please,' Theo said, thinking of the journey home.

'Join us when you're finished,' said Jeanette over her shoulder as she disappeared through the doorway, her arm linked with Martin's. Theo packed up her things, swept the area around the tree and fumed, then she was angry for feeling out of sorts with herself and with everyone else suddenly.

Chapter Six

Martin built the fire while Theo made peace with Cat who greedily took the offering of prawns. With Cat satisfied, Theo set about organising dinner, still a bit resentful. It wasn't that she didn't want to spend time with Martin, it was more that it was now. She didn't remember hearing him say he was coming but that may have been because she had shut down after his concern about her being on her own for Christmas. He, above all people, shouldn't try and meddle with her life. He was a priest and should understand the need for solitude.

As she brought a bottle of wine through to the sitting room and saw him in front of the fire, she forgave him everything. He was a good man and had devoted his life to others much as their father had done. Martin had just taken a more radical route, becoming a Jesuit whereas their father had been a kindly Anglican vicar.

'What news do you have from our mother?' He stood and took the bottle and corkscrew from her.

'She's in Oxford and has found a man.'

He smirked. 'I trust he's wealthy.'

'Hasn't she been in touch with you?'

'Minimal. Must be she's afraid to say she's living in sin.' He pulled the cork out and they both laughed. Their mother had always been more virtuous than anyone and now she was living with a man who was four years her junior. She had been scathing about Theo's divorce and the subsequent revelation that David hadn't been Piers's son after all. It had taken much coaxing on Martin's part to suggest Theo forgive her and move on.

During the course of the lockdown she had emailed her mother and Virginia had replied. Theo wouldn't call it normal but at least they were communicating. In truth Theo was pleased for her mother. It surprised her though that Virginia hadn't been in contact with her beloved son. Martin wasn't one to pass judgement but more to talk about God's love being limitless. Martin should know since he had a PhD in physics. Theo was the one who was a bit unsure but that, according to her mother, was because she was under-educated and had never applied herself.

'I'm afraid aside from a few vegetables it's a cold meal tonight.'

'I won't complain.' He followed her into the kitchen. Together they gathered the food and bought it through to the table in the sitting room. Cat eyed them with suspicion. The feline did not care for quiche and was not impressed with potatoes or carrots. Instead after her inspection she settled on a cushion near the fire. Every time Theo looked at the fireplace she felt the history of her little home. Back in the eighteen hundreds it was built with the sole purpose to have rising smoke visible from Abbotswood when the hotel was a hunting lodge for the Dukes of Exeter. Who were, fate would have it, hers and Martin's forebears. Sometimes it still felt to strange to believe. Yet around her neck hung her grandmother's engagement ring linking it all together.

'So tell me what's bothering you,' Martin said pouring the wine.

Theo sent him a look.

'Do I have to dig under the floorboards to find your journal these days?'

'Ha,' she said. Theo dived into the kitchen as her face flared. He'd read all her diaries. He knew all about Paris. She heard his phone ring and she leaned against the counter. Paris.

It was ten o'clock in the evening, a month before her wedding, and she'd had far too much wine and laughed until her stomach hurt. On the longest day of the year, the lights of Paris were just coming on. Darkness wouldn't fall until later. At that point she would turn into a pumpkin, no she was muddling things. Theo would be who she actually was, Theodora Grace Pascoe engaged to Piers Henshaw. But right in this moment she was Theo. And it was a glorious thing to be with the sexiest man she had ever met or was ever likely to meet. Above her the first star of the evening glimmered.

Theo searched for others and found Patrick had wrapped his arms around her to steady her. She looked into his eyes instead of at the stars. Her glance fell to his mouth. She reached up and touched his bottom lip. His smile was beautiful and his breath smelled of pink wine. Theo leaned in, wanting. Was he going to pull away? His arms held her a bit closer. She tiptoed, placed her lips against his and waited, unsure. His mouth moved. He said her name. She kissed him and her own hunger surprised her. The horn from a boat sounded but they didn't stop. Everything in her longed to be closer to him. He drew back and studied her. He missed nothing. 'Let's go back to my place and have some more wine.'

Theo nodded. She didn't need more wine, but she wanted him like she had never wanted anyone before. It throbbed within her. The lightest touch from Patrick set off a reaction. She needed to explode and that would only be possible with him. His fingers laced through her and she shivered.

'Sorry about that.' Martin walked back into the kitchen. 'You were telling me about you?'

'I'm good.' She led the way back to their dinner. 'I'm busy and I'm enjoying having my house back.'

'Really?'

'Yes, I miss the three of them, but I see them most weeks which is more than Natasha's parents do.' She helped herself to the carrots and potatoes and pushed the bowls towards Martin.

'You're isolated here.'

'Not really. The hotel is just across the river and more importantly I'm happy here.'

He held his hands up. 'I wasn't suggesting you move just that you're isolated.'

'I work most days seeing many people. I have good friends.'

'Agree on all of that.'

'Then what is this about?' she asked.

'You, and the fact that you are fifty-eight and alone.'

Theo drew a deep breath. Not him too. No one understood that she was happy alone. 'Just don't go there Martin. Not you who has chosen a life of celibacy.'

He leaned back in his chair. A smile played about his mouth. He was so damned handsome he must break a hundred hearts a day. 'Fair point but my life is full.'

'So is mine.'

'Is it?' He took a sip of his wine. 'From where I'm sitting you are now actively avoiding love.'

She would not take this conversation seriously.

'It's been a couple of years since the divorce, albeit strange years, and it's time you stepped back out into the world and into love.'

'I don't choose well when it comes to love.' She ran her finger along the grain of the wooden table.

'Patrick sounded like he was the right choice.'

48

She twisted the wine glass in her fingers. 'He may have been but I didn't stay.'

'Circumstances stepped in and took over.'

She snorted a laugh. 'Doesn't say much for me.'

'Love is a positive choice, and you are a positive person.'

'I don't need that type of love in my life.' She put down her fork. 'Did Jeanette put you up to this?'

'No.' He shook his head.

'You will always be a shit liar.'

He laughed. 'She did mention there was a suitable candidate in the neighbourhood.'

Theo put her head into her hands. Erik. The poor man was here to help his son and he was being set up by her well-meaning friends. She would have to apologise to him when she saw him next at the workshop on Friday.

'Enough. Tell me about what's up in your life?' She topped up their glasses of wine.

'Teaching mostly. That hasn't changed.' He paused. 'Is that your phone ringing?'

Theo dashed into the kitchen. 'Hello,' she answered a bit breathless.

'Hi Theo. Sorry to ring so late but wanted to let you know I have to cancel.'

'Oh.' Theo blinked. Nathan was her biggest client and it was all set for a three day operation next week and she had purchased everything to dress his house for Christmas.

'Don't worry, it's last minute so I will pay the full fee.'

'Are you OK?' Theo raced through the options that could cause such a short term cancellation. None of them were good.

'Yes, more than OK. Isabelle has just proposed, and we are off to get married in the Caribbean.'

'Fabulous, congrats!' Theo sank against the counter in relief.

'I never thought I'd find love at sixty-five.' He chuckled. 'It's great, you should try it.'

'Not you too,' Theo said out loud. 'Sorry, that wasn't meant for you.' She quickly covered her outburst. She must become less sensitive to this subject.

'Have a happy Christmas Theo. I've transferred the funds to your account.'

'Thank you, and huge congrats to you both!' She put the phone down. What on earth was she going to do with the trees, wreaths and decor?

'You look like you need something stronger than a glass of wine.'

'I do.'

Martin went to the bottle of single malt whisky on the side table and poured them both a small measure. He handed the glass to her. Watching the candlelight flicker in the amber liquid, she acknowledged the gaping hole in her schedule. What was she going to do with the five extra days between prep and set up that was now in her diary? She could offer David another couple of days of childcare. That would fill the gap nicely.

Chapter Seven

Theo had dropped her car off at the garage and hitched a lift with Gayle, and now she stood in the stable yard not sure how it had come to be Friday already. She touched the ears of the little rabbit in her pocket, thinking how Martin's time with her had flown by. It had turned out he was a dab hand at talking to couples about to marry. While she focused on their floral desires, he spoke to them about their relationships. They actually made a good team, talking about dreams for the day and dreams for the future.

'Morning gorgeous,' Tim said, walking towards her with two steaming coffees.

'Morning.' Theo smiled and held out a hand. 'Thank you.'

'Are you glum because your brother has gone?' He opened the function room in the stables building.

'A little. He's good company but I'll enjoy the cottage to myself this weekend.'

Tim didn't say a word but nodded with a wide-eyed look on his face. The cheek of him. They were all against her. No, she corrected herself. They were all for her, thinking they knew what was best. She took a sip of coffee. It was all a question of how you looked at things. They loved her and that was all that mattered.

'A full house today,' Tim laid out the frames on the table in front of the sixteen seats. 'And of course Erik will be here.'

'Am already,' Erik said, carrying a plate. 'I brought some pepparkakor for you both.'

Theo could smell the cinnamon and cloves as he neared her with the thin biscuits, cut into hearts and stars.

'Yum.' Tim took a star and looked from the plate to Theo challenging her to take a heart. He was a wicked soul. She picked up a heart simply to meet his challenge and bit into it. The spices and sweetness hit her taste buds.

'These are delicious.' She grinned and studied Erik. 'Did you make them?'

'I did, from my grandmother's recipe.' He picked up a biscuit. 'I have always found cooking a great relaxation.'

'When can you move in?' Tim asked, taking another. 'I hate cooking.'

'Shame. Such a simple pleasure.' He glanced at Theo.

'I enjoy it, but baking has never been my strong point.' Theo resisted taking another and sipped her coffee instead.

'I could show you. It's really quite simple.' He took a heart shaped one for himself. 'Most important is to measure your ingredients carefully.'

'Don't tell me.' Tim rolled his eyes. 'You're an engineer or architect.'

'How did you know?' Erik bit into his biscuit.

'The measuring of ingredients.' Tim stole another. 'I've watched Theo cook and she barely glances at a recipe. It's all instinct and feel for the ingredients with her. She's a bit like that with flowers too.'

Theo was about to object but instinct was a key feature in both her design and her cooking.

'I agree instinct is important, especially on flavours, but if the balance of ingredients isn't correct you will have what you call a soggy bottom.'

The way the words sounded in his slightly accented English were almost as delicious as his cookies. Her mouth twitched. 'You watch *The Great British Bake Off*?'

'Of course. I've surprised you?'

'You have.' She couldn't resist any longer. The biscuits smelled too good. She took another, hoping it wouldn't taste as good as the first one.

'Good.' His eyes crinkled in the corners.

Theo wanted to look away but instead asked, 'Why is that good?'

'It is best not to be too predictable.' A slow smile spread across his face. Theo swallowed. She shouldn't find him so attractive. It wasn't good for clear thinking.

'Too true,' said Tim.

Theo's phone rang. It was David, so she excused herself and stepped aside. 'Morning darling,' she said, only a little concerned since this wasn't normal. This was a morning when Zach was with a minder and he was painting.

'Mum, can you do me a huge favour?'

'I can try.'

'The minder has just tested positive for Covid and I'm due in London for Tash's work's Christmas shindig in three hours. I can't let her down.'

'You want me to come and look after Zach?'

'Yes, please.' She heard the relief in his voice.

'Damn.' The swear slipped out of her. 'I don't have a car. It's in for repairs.'

'Bugger.' He paused. 'I need to be on that train.'

'Is everything alright? Surely Natasha will understand.'

'Um, no.' He sighed. 'Look, we had a bit of an argument last night.'

'Oh.' Theo glanced at Tim. 'Let me see if I can borrow a car.'

Tim looked up. 'What's mine is yours.'

'Your car?'

'Of course,' he said then his face fell. 'Sadly not today though. Mum dropped me off this morning. Mine is having new front brakes installed.'

Theo closed her eyes. She needed to help.

'Can I drive you somewhere?' Erik asked.

'Mum, this is serious.' He drew a breath. 'I wouldn't ask if it wasn't.'

'I know.' She paused, glancing at Erik. If she wanted to help David and she did, she would have to accept Erik's offer. 'Give me two minutes and I'll find a solution. Get ready.'

'OK. We'll be back by ten at the latest since this is an afternoon, early evening thing.'

Theo put the phone down and picked up a copper frame for the course.

'Don't worry about this.' Tim waved his hand at the table. 'I've got it covered and you can give Erik private tuition and lunch another time.' He winked at her. She hoped that Erik hadn't seen it and hadn't heard the innuendo in Tim's voice.

'I'm happy to help.' Erik walked to her side.

Theo looked into his eyes. They were smiling at her and she was tempted. 'But it will be the whole day babysitting and it won't finish until late.'

Erik shrugged. 'That's fine as I don't have to be anywhere else.'

'Thank you,' She laid her hand on his arm for a moment then called David and said she was on her way.

'Don't worry about me or the students today.' Tim gave her a hug. 'We'll have a ball.'

Theo picked up her backpack and followed Erik out of the

stables. 'This is very kind,' she said, noting the Swedish license plates on his car.

'Happy to help.' He opened the door for her.

'You brought your car with you?'

'Yes, at first I intended this as a surprise for Oskar but in the end that wasn't possible.'

'So he knows you are finishing the house?' Theo fitted her seatbelt.

'He does.'

She turned to him. 'And he is pleased?'

'Yes,' he said, starting the engine. 'For him it means it will be easier to sell.'

'Oh.'

Erik took a deep breath. 'It will break my heart if he, at the age of thirty-five, shuts life out and only lives to work. Love is available to him again.'

Theo nodded but was not sure she agreed, thinking of her grandmother, Claire.

'I can see you are not truly of the same opinion, but you are too polite to say it.' He manoeuvred the car onto the lane. 'You have an expressive face.' He glanced from her to the road.

'I believe sometimes we are lucky to have love once and that is enough.'

'Is it enough?'

Theo looked at the winter landscape around her. The architecture of the trees was visible and in their unadorned state the wind could rattle through them causing less harm. She shivered. 'I think it is.'

'You loved once and don't plan to again?'

'Yes.' It was strange to say this to a man she barely knew. Her brief time with Patrick must sustain her.

'I thought this too and threw myself into my work to fill the aching void.' He shrugged. 'But it was not a creative joyous work like you do. Although I enjoy the design and build process, I ended up in management, climbing high and far away from what drew me to the field.'

'I can see how that could happen.'

'In a way I lost Oskar and my time with him by doing that. He stayed in Sweden with my sister and came to me during the holidays. It wasn't enough.' Erik turned out onto the dual carriageway. 'I lost his mother and I lost both myself and my son. She would have been so disappointed.'

Theo reached out and placed her hand lightly on his arm. She knew the pain of regret. 'But you are now trying to help your son and I'm certain that she would be pleased.'

He glanced at her. 'I like to think so.'

The morning's clear skies clouded over and by the time they were nearing Exeter the rain was falling with gusto. She hoped the weather would be better in London for David and that his journey would mend whatever they had argued about.

Chapter Eight

David's face was the picture of relief when he opened the door. His eyebrows nearly disappeared when he spied Erik behind Theo. Her sense of relief was huge that David had no time for a chat because she saw the questions lurking on David's lips when he jumped into a waiting taxi.

Her grandson's little face was full of smiles as she scooped him up and took him straight to the kitchen. Lunchtime would soon be upon them and she knew how quickly Zach's mood could change if he wasn't fed. Once he was secured in the high chair, Theo rummaged in the cupboards for some quick fix baby food. At Boatman's her freezer was laden with ice cube-sized chunks of puréed food. Nothing like puréed chicken and peas followed by sieved apple to set a boy straight.

She perched on the nearest chair to Zach while Erik filled the kettle. Within minutes she had a mug of tea and a biscuit to keep her going.

Zach's head began to drop once he had finished his lunch so she grabbed a clean cloth and tidied his messy hands and face. She took him from the high chair and smiled at Erik as he turned from studying one of David's paintings.

After a quick nappy change, Zach settled for a long overdue

nap. He was asleep almost as soon as his head rested on the mattress. She placed a light blanket over him and checked the baby monitor was switched on. That done she could see what there was in the kitchen to give Erik a bite to eat, as the biscuits wouldn't sustain either of them.

'Sleeping?' Erik asked as Theo entered the kitchen.

'Almost before he was in the cot.' She headed towards the fridge. 'Now I'll see if I can find us some sort of lunch.'

'Thank you. May I help?'

'The plates are in the cupboard and the cutlery in the drawer below.'

There was a cry from the baby monitor and Theo raced back to her grandson's bedroom. The problem was obvious. The beloved teddy was on the floor. She picked it up and tucked it next to Zach, who then closed his eyes and nuzzled into the bear's tummy. Stationary for a while, she watched the rise and fall of Zach's chest as he fell soundly back to sleep, then she tiptoed out of the room.

In the kitchen, she smelled soup and saw Erik making a salad.

'You didn't have to.' The table was laid and he had found an apron emblazoned with the words 'Not just a pretty face'. She swallowed a smile.

'I'm hungry.' He brought the salad to the table.

'Me too.' She took a seat.

'Please start. I'm just grabbing the bread from the oven.' He placed it on the board in the centre of the table and sliced a few pieces off.

'This is wonderful and thank you again for dropping every-thing and coming to my aid, or rather to David's.'

'I had no plans other than making a wreath.'

'Oh God.' Theo blew on a spoonful of soup. 'I'd completely forgotten about the course. I'll refund you, and one morning this week you could come by and make another wreath.'

'That would be good.'

'I couldn't have come without your help.'

'Happy I could assist.' His eyes twinkled with mischief. He was, as the apron said, a pretty face and a very attractive man in all senses. Not that she was looking, but he was worth appreciating, especially that smile and those blue eyes. He must have been very blond in his youth, for his grey hair had that silvery tint that blonds usually go.

'How much work is left on your son's house?' she asked.

'It's all the . . .' he raised his hands.

'In the UK we use the term "snagging" for all the small jobs that are unfinished.'

'Good word.' He tore a piece of bread in half. 'I have a long snagging list and I'm also trying to make it festive.'

'You can hide many unfinished things with decorations.' She ate a bite of her salad.

'You can, and I have.' The corner of his mouth lifted in a half-smile that she found incredibly sexy. 'It is a beautiful house but very remote.'

'Old?' she asked, trying to think of anything but the man sitting in front of her.

'Georgian.'

'Glorious windows and lovely lines.' She added silently, just like you.

He nodded. 'The views across the moor are stunning.'

A happy cooing sound emitted from the monitor.

'Shall I check him?' Erik asked.

'He's fine for another few minutes.' Theo finished her salad and hopped to her feet as the first grumble was heard. The volume had increased by the time she reached Zach's bedroom but he stopped as soon as he saw her.

'Hello, little one,' she whispered, sniffing the air to see if a nappy change was required, but no unpleasant smell confronted her. She scooped him up and gave him a cuddle, loving the way he held on and looked up at her. Who knew she could feel so much love for another small human. Her heart could burst with it.

She was walking back to the kitchen when her phone rang. Erik opened his arms and took Zach so she could answer it.

She quelled the panic when she saw the number. 'David? All OK?'

'Yes, just checking on you and wanted to say thank you again.' She could hear the relaxed tone of his voice and knew that things were much better.

'Glad I could help.'

'By the way, who is the man?' David asked.

Theo laughed. That was the real reason for the call. Curiosity. 'He's a student of mine.'

'Really?'

'Yes, really.'

'You know Mum, you can have a man in your life and that is fine with me.'

She coughed. 'That's definitely good to know, but this is not that.'

'If you're sure,' he pressed.

'Positive.'

'We're about to head into the event. I'll text you with our ETA later.'

'Have a wonderful time,' she said.

'Love you.'

'Love you too.' The phone line cut out.

Theo went in search of Erik and Zach and found them sitting on the floor playing with Zach's favourite coloured blocks. Erik was building towers and Zach gleefully knocking them down. She left them to it and looked into a near empty fridge, then went to the utility room. In the freezer she found a lasagna and put it on the side to defrost then she joined Zach and Erik on the floor and built her own tower of blocks.

Chapter Nine

Theo woke up as Erik's car hit a rut. She snorted in the most unladylike fashion and quickly mumbled, 'Sorry.'

'A nap is always a good thing.'

She cleared her throat. 'Not good for directing you or keeping you company.'

'Have I found the right place?' He asked.

Caught in his headlights Boatman's looked enchanting. Cat on the other hand appeared wet and grumpy sitting on the doorstep.

'Can I offer you a drink?' Theo asked.

'That would be nice.' He turned off the engine and they both left the car.

It was only nine thirty because David and Natasha had caught the earlier train. There were no signs of the argument that David had mentioned. One thing Theo had done was to compliment Natasha on the Christmas tree and other decorations around the house. Natasha had sent her an odd look, but Theo had been genuine in her compliment. It was important for Natasha and David to have their own Christmas and to do it their way without her or her shadow hanging over it.

Theo walked towards the cottage and wished she had put

the lights on a timer as it would seem more welcoming. Cat snaked through Theo's legs bitterly complaining. The feline abandoned Theo and looked up at Erik who bent and scratched her head. *Traitor*, thought Theo as she unlocked the door.

'Is this the welcoming committee?' he asked.

'She wants food and a dry bed.'

'Good things to want.' He said as Cat squeezed into the house before the door was fully open.

Inside Theo switched the light on. Cat circled back and wove through Erik's legs. She clearly thought he was a softer touch. He bent down to the cat. 'Your cat is very beautiful.'

'She is and she knows it.' Theo cast the cat a glance then headed into the kitchen calling over her shoulder, 'Make yourself comfortable but don't let her sit on you as she's wet.'

'Too late,' he replied. 'What is her name?'

'Cat.'

'Yes, you mentioned that.' Erik looked up from the feline he was stroking.

'Not very imaginative but she arrived at Boatman's the same time I did and I was certain she had an owner somewhere. Long story short, she didn't, and I'd been calling her Cat for lack of another name and it stuck.' She paused. 'Would you like a glass of wine, a hot drink?'

He sighed. 'I have a forty minute drive in front of me so a hot drink it is.' He followed her into the kitchen. 'I love the wooden panels. Just like the hotel.'

'They are beautiful, aren't they?'

He turned to Theo and his glance met hers. 'Yes.'

She swallowed. He wasn't looking at the panelling but at her. She had gone past the point of beauty. She was interesting now, at least that was what she told herself when she looked in the mirror.

She turned from him and asked, 'Tea or coffee?'

'Tea, herbal if you have it, please.'

'I do. Camomile? Or I have fresh mint?' Theo took two mugs down from the open shelves.

'Fresh mint.' He ran his hand over the scarred wooden surface of her kitchen table. 'This is a lovely piece of furniture.' He looked up. 'It speaks of many meals and activity.'

'It belonged to my grandmother.' A lump formed in her throat. Gone since 2018 and Theo still missed her.

'And you loved her.'

'Very much.'

'I can tell by the way your eyes lit up when you thought of her.'

'I miss her, but it was her time.' Theo paused. 'If you'll excuse me I'll just nip into the greenhouse and grab some mint.'

'May I come? I love greenhouses.'

'Of course but it's more of a lean-to than a full-blown greenhouse.'

'Oskar's house has the remains of one in the walled kitchen garden and I long to see it repaired.'

'Is it a large one?'

'It covers three quarters of the southwest wall.'

'For peaches and tomatoes.' She turned on the light and walked down the hall leading to the back door and her little greenhouse. 'The aroma would have been wonderful.'

'Not too bad in here either.' He looked about as she gathered some mint.

'That's the mahonia just outside you're smelling.' She pointed to the plant scaling the bricks at the base of the grass. 'Shall we go and sit in the other room and I can light the fire.'

'Cat will appreciate it,' he said, stroking the animal who rubbed against his legs. Theo raised an eyebrow at Cat's clear signposting of her approval. She was as bad as Tim.

Theo poured the hot water on the mint leaves and set about lighting the fire while the tea brewed. Erik scanned the bookshelves and studied the pictures. Once the fire was alight she

63

gathered the tea from the kitchen and handed Erik a mug before sitting in one of the armchairs.

Cat had settled on Erik's lap as soon as he sat. Theo called her a traitor again silently, but couldn't blame Cat as Erik scratched behind her ears. She might even be a bit jealous. Before she could let her thoughts go any further down that road she said, 'Thank you again for your help.'

His eyes sought hers. 'It was a pleasure.'

She took a sip of her tea and leaned back into the chair. The cottage seemed to settle around them both.

'Your home is beautiful.'

She looked at the wood panels gleaming in the firelight. 'I love it. It took time and a lot of hard work but I am pleased with the results.'

'You did the work yourself?' he asked.

She nodded. 'Does that surprise you?'

'Not in the sense that I did not think you could do the work, but more . . . ' He drew a breath. 'There's no way to dig myself out of this, is there?'

Theo laughed. 'No, there isn't but it was entertaining watching you try.'

'Had you done this type of work before?'

'Years ago on a big house.' With a big budget Theo added silently. 'Are you enjoying the work on your son's house?'

'Loving it,' he said. 'I only wish he was doing it with me.'

'It's hard being a parent. One walks minefields all the time between being loving and trying to be helpful, yet not stepping on toes.'

'Am I wrong in sensing that Natasha thought you were being untruthful about her decorations?'

Theo put her mug down. 'You don't miss much.'

'No.' The corner of his mouth lifted in that appealing way again. Theo's stomach tightened.

'Last year we had Christmas here. She was exhausted and I did everything.'

'And you are a professional.'

'Yes, so she feels insecure, but she has no reason to.' Theo cradled her mug. 'That's why I am letting them have their own Christmas without me.'

'Not to avoid the in-laws?'

Theo shook her head. 'They are lovely, and I had David, Natasha and Zach all to myself last year, so they deserve the opportunity. And David and Natasha need to make their own traditions.'

He looked about the room. 'I see you haven't decorated.'

'No, I'm planning a quiet Christmas.'

He tilted his head and studied her. 'If that's what you wish then it is good.'

'It is.'

A disbelieving smile played across his mouth and Theo resisted the urge to lean across the gap between them and kiss him. Instead she turned and studied the dancing flames and the fire, but that didn't cool her thoughts either.

Her phone pinged. She leaped to her feet grateful for the distraction. It was a text from David.

All well here. Thanks for saving my ass. Xx

She quickly typed, walking into the kitchen.

Same here.

The reply was swift.

Your friend Erik seems a good sort.

Theo looked through to the man sitting at ease in her grand-mother's old armchair then typed.

He is.

Theo collected the teapot and walked back to the sitting room. 'More tea?'

'Yes, please.' He held the empty mug out to her and Cat sent her a look for disturbing her rest.

Theo filled her own mug and sat down.

'Tell me about your family,' he said. 'I know you have a son and a grandson. Any other children?'

'David is my only one.' She looked at him. 'Is Oskar your only child?'

'Yes, he is.'

'Do you have siblings?' she asked.

'One sister lives in New York and the other in Stockholm. What about you?'

'My brother is a physicist and Jesuit priest and my mother . . .' Theo made a face.

'Which one don't you like?'

She laughed. 'My brother is wonderful.'

'I see,' he said and she could see he did. 'Your father?'

'Sadly no longer with us. He was a vicar and the kindest person.'

'Like you.'

'I am not in his league.' She laughed. 'Your parents?'

'They have been gone for a while.' He sighed.

'Hard,' she said and to lift the sadness that had settled on them both, she asked, 'How long do you plan on staying in Cornwall?'

'I imagine until taking down day.'

'The sixth of January?'

'No, in Sweden it is later in the month.'

Theo closed her eyes for a moment. 'If I'd decorated this year, I'd leave the decorations up longer, but tradition and superstition keep me on time.'

'You don't strike me as superstitious.'

'I'm not but I am.' She shrugged and took a sip of tea. 'Things are good and I wouldn't want to tempt fate.'

'Always a good thing to stay on fortune's side.'

'What will you do when you return to Sweden?' she asked.

'I don't know.' He scratched between Cat's ears. 'I might travel. I might sail.'

'Nothing to tie you down?' She tried to imagine his life but she had so little to go on.

'No, I have a lock up and leave apartment.'

Theo looked around her. She couldn't imagine leaving Boatman's.

'Older houses are harder to leave,' he said. 'And you are by the water in a place of such beauty.'

'It is and I have a wonderful community.'

'Jeanette, Tim, Hugo and Gayle and others.' He put his mug down. It was empty again.

'More?' she asked.

'I'll pass but I would love to another time.' He smiled then stifled a yawn as he stood with Cat complaining loudly.

She rose to her feet, not wanting him to leave. This was a new feeling and she didn't want to examine it. 'Thank you again for your help today.'

'I was glad to.' He collected his coat and Cat lifted her head to accept another neck scratch. 'I'll see you tomorrow morning at the workshop if you are there.'

'I will be, and we can sort out making you another wreath,' she said and walked him to the door. The night had cleared and the sky was filled with stars.

'A shooting star,' they said at the same time.

'I hope you made a wish,' She lowered her glance from the heavens.

He looked directly at her and said, 'I did.'

'Me too.' But she couldn't remember or wouldn't admit even to herself what she had wished for. Instead she watched Erik walk to his car and found herself smiling.

Chapter Ten

Theo relaxed and noted that all the wreaths were complete and participants were settling down to their lunch. Erik was engaged in an earnest discussion with one of the women on the course who was making eyes at him. Jealousy surged and Theo immediately bit it back. She wasn't involved with him and wouldn't be, but she wasn't honest if she didn't admit that the idea had crossed her mind.

Hugo came up to her and she followed him through the courtyard. It was something about the wedding she was certain. Outside, the rain had begun softening the edges of the buildings and giving it a fairy tale quality with the fairy lights sparkling.

Once they were in the entrance hall, he put his hand in his pocket, pulled out a box and opened it. A sapphire and diamond eternity ring glistened in the dull December light.

'You can't propose to me, you're already engaged.'

Hugo laughed. 'Do you think she'll like it?'

'Yes. It's elegant and beautiful and very Gayle.'

'She can't wear her engagement ring every day working in the garden so I thought this might work as a wedding ring.'

'May I?' Theo asked.

'Of course.'

She lifted the ring out of the box. The white gold was cold in her hands. 'It's beautiful.'

'I'm having it engraved.'

Theo tilted her her head, waiting.

He cleared his throat. 'A most constant heart.' He flushed.

She touched his hand sensing his embarrassment at showing his feelings to others. 'Beautiful.' Love, she knew it once and was delighted to see it around her in this couple and in David's life. Her stomach hollowed for a moment thinking of her lost years but one couldn't go back and fix the past. Only the future could be helped.

'I won't keep you, but thought you could tell me if the ring was practical enough for every day in the garden.'

'It is, and as long as she has the settings checked each year it should be fine.'

Theo touched her grandmother's emerald ring hanging on a chain around her neck. It was not practical at all but it was a thing of beauty. It was too big for real life but Theo couldn't sell it therefore she wore it near her heart to remind her of her grandmother, Claire.

'I'd better check on my workshop.'

Hugo set off to his office and Theo strolled back to the workshop to discover Tim on his way to her.

'There you are. I just took a call from potential clients for a wedding in the summer and booked it in your diary.'

'Thank you.' Together they went through the courtyard and skirted the greenery covering the surface of half of it.

'I also noted that Nathan had cancelled and have booked another client in.'

She frowned. 'For dressing a house?'

'Yes.' He tucked his arm through hers in a conspiratorial way.

Theo stopped. 'But I don't know the requirements.'

'No worries on that account, you can meet with him after lunch.'

'He's coming here?'

'Already here. It's Erik.'

She stared at Tim.

'No need to give me that "mother disapproves" look. He needs help and you have the time.'

Theo rolled her eyes. Matchmaking. He may not think so, but she could see through his plan, and it wasn't going to work.

Erik walked up to her with an apologetic smile on his face. 'I'm sorry. Is it inconvenient for you to help me?'

What could she say to that? It was inconvenient because she found him attractive. 'I thought you had it all under control?'

'I did until the painter came down with Covid this morning, therefore I am painting and not decorating.'

'I see.' It all made sense. She understood the desire to do anything for your child. 'Then of course I can help.'

'Good.' He picked up his wreath.

'I will need a brief from you.'

His eyes crinkled with his smile. 'It is Swedish meets English.'

She laughed. 'Guess I need to Google Swedish Christmas traditions.'

'Or I could tell you.' That sexy half-smile appeared again.

'What a brilliant idea.' Tim beamed. 'I can handle the clean-up here, and you two could go and find a quiet spot in the hotel to discuss it all.' He placed a hand on Theo's back and pushed her towards Erik and the door.

'OK, but what about—'

'I'll take care of everything,' Tim said with a wink.

She could throttle him but instead she followed Erik through the courtyard and into the hotel. They went to the library where the fire was lit and before she could ask, Hugo brought a pot of tea.

71

Pulling out her notebook, she looked at her new client and her normal questions flew out of her mind. Where did she begin? 'What have you achieved so far?'

'I have two wreaths and two trees.' He smiled sheepishly. Today was the eleventh of December.

'You have lights and ornaments?' At Martin's suggestions she had donated Nathan's trees and decorations to a homeless shelter.

'I don't.' He leaned back in the chair as Theo poured the tea. She handed him a cup and recalled the almost bare shelves she had seen at the supermarkets and the things in the garden centre had already been well picked over by the start of the month. She looked at the lights on the tree thinking even if they didn't find the decorations, lights were essential. This time of year lights made a huge difference.

'Have you set a budget?'

'No.' He shook his head. 'I will spend whatever it takes.'

'You really want to make this work for your son.'

'I do. I need him to open up again, even if it is just for a day.' He stared out the window towards the river. 'I threw away many years not living but grieving. I don't want him to do the same.'

This she understood. For years she marked time, not living. She must have looked like such a fool to everyone, but she had refused to see it, thinking it was for the best.

Picking up a biscuit an idea arrived. 'Shall we head to Exeter tomorrow?'

'To see your family?' He asked.

'That would be a bonus but there is a large store there known for its meatballs, and they may have things we will need to transform the house into a blend of English and Swedish.'

He laughed. 'Would you like to see the house first?'

'Yes, after we finish this cup shall we head off?'

'Of course.'

Theo may have been tricked into doing this job by Tim but she also couldn't resist the opportunity to see a house being renovated and the challenge of delivering Christmas.

* * *

The journey to the house was longer than she expected. The last habitable dwelling was miles ago but as she followed Erik's car through the gates, her skin tingled. The lines of the house were divine and appeared un-doctored. All around were rough fields and vistas across the moors. A striking tor loomed nearby. She parked by the stables, and it was clear from her first glance that the house was set in a slight dip to provide a bit of protection from the weather. Once out of her car, the chill of the air circled her. There would be a frost tonight. She would have to be careful driving home.

Erik waited by the low stone wall that divided the garden at the front of the house and the gravel drive. The house was perfection while the garden was in need of love and her fingers twitched. The planting would have to be carefully planned, for the weather would be more severe, but it would be magical.

'What do you think?' He waited for her to join him.

'I love it.'

'It's special.' He held out a hand directing her to the front door. Erik's first wreath hung on it, looking beautiful on the soft blue paint. The house was solidly built of granite and the wooden sash windows were painted in the same blue as the door which softened the stern feel of the stone. She looked over her shoulder at the vista. The browns and reds of the bracken glowed golden in the low afternoon light. It took her breath away. She had become so used to the densely wooded views of the riverside that she had missed out on the large vistas of the moors so close both in Cornwall and Devon. Had she been too cocooned or was that just a result of the crazy world they had been living in? No, everyone had been only existing. Living meant grabbing life with both hands and embracing it. She had been doing just that when the world had shut down.

'Where have you gone?' Erik asked.

'Sorry, away with the fairies, as they say.'

His glance narrowed.

'I guess that doesn't translate.' She smiled. 'I was lost in my thoughts.'

'We would say, I was in a world of my own.' He opened the front door. 'Welcome to Gwen an Hal, which means "moor view" in Cornish, I'm told.'

Theo drank in every detail. The large slate flagstones, the white painted wainscoting and the modern sleek pendant light which worked because of the stark contrast. The blending of old and new felt easy as did the warmth of the house. This she wasn't used to, in an old house filled with tall ceilings, single glazed windows and dodgy boilers. That was the one thing she had never succeeded at, despite the money that her ex had put into their old home.

The first room off the hallway was half finished. She spied the paint pots and drop cloths in all the rooms they passed. The kitchen was complete. She was so impressed with the vision for the house. It respected the old but embraced the new.

'How do you keep it so warm?'

'Ground pump and solar.' He filled the kettle. 'As you can see I have much to do before Christmas Eve when Oskar is coming.' He frowned.

'Is something wrong?'

He switched the kettle on. 'In the past we would decorate the tree the day before Christmas Eve but Oskar has work commitments and can't get away until the day itself.'

Theo placed a hand on his arm.

'It's fine. At least he is coming.' He smiled.

Theo glanced around, excited to start. 'Have you made a list?'

He laughed. 'A spreadsheet. I'm an engineer.'

'Fair point.' She looked around. 'You mentioned you have Christmas trees.'

'Outside and in pots of water.'

'Good.' She opened her notebook. 'So you have two trees and two wreaths.'

'That is all.' He pulled out two large mugs.

'The house is beautiful and it won't take much to make it festive.' The clean modern lines of the kitchen wouldn't require much either.

He raised an eyebrow.

'Trust me.'

'I do.' He looked her directly in the eyes. Her breath hitched.

She spun around. 'May I have a wander?'

'Of course. Make yourself at home.'

'Thank you.' She fled to avoid making eye contact again.

'I'll make a pot of tea and open the spreadsheet so we can add your items,' he called.

'Great,' she replied, noting there were four large rooms to the front of the house on either side of the hallway. The dining room faced north-west and had wide floorboards that looked original. A first coat of red paint covered the walls while both the ceiling and the skirting board were white. The large table was covered in a dust sheet. Erik had his work cut out if he was going to finish by Christmas. The morning room opposite had the paint from the previous occupant of the house which was best described as mouldy green. She escaped that and went into what would become the library, judging by the shelves and the boxes of books piled in the middle of the room. The white gloss work was fresh and the walls primed. She stood for a moment enjoying the view westward, framed in the tall windows.

Across the hall she only peeked in the sitting room which wasn't finished either. Upstairs, she hoped for Erik's sake things were further along. She found two large bedrooms complete with fully fitted en suites at the front of the house. They were beautifully done and furnished again with a mix of antique and modern. All that was missing were paintings or some wall art. Perhaps Erik was leaving that to Oskar.

There were a further five bedrooms and, like the downstairs rooms, they were fully prepped for transformation. The work on the many bathrooms was complete.

As she walked down the back staircase, Theo sighed. Now that Boatman's was done she missed working on a property. But there were other challenges she could take on to fill the void.

She arrived back in the kitchen where Erik was sitting at the table with his laptop open. He looked up smiling at her and she almost lost her footing. She wasn't supposed to feel this at fifty-eight.

'What did you think?' He tapped the seat beside him.

'I love it, but there's no way you will have it finished by Christmas.'

His shoulders dropped a bit. 'I know.'

'But what is done . . . is stunning.'

'Thank you.'

'What is your plan?' She asked, sitting and accepting a cup of tea.

'There is nothing else I can do to the kitchen.' He pointed to the glasshouse style extension. 'That requires professionals to finish, but I can paint walls and woodwork as well as sand the bottom of the wooden shutters and adjust their heights.'

'The latter is impressive.' She had admired the original shutters in all the windows.

He shrugged. 'Years of making things fit in awkward places.'

'I could help with the painting,' she suggested.

'Really?'

She grabbed her bag and pulled out her diary. She had three houses to dress this coming week. If she asked Sue to join her and Tim, Theo could be sure of finishing them quickly. 'We can shop for decorations and ideas on Monday.' She ran her fingers over the diary page. She was helping her cousin Toby tomorrow. 'Then I will be free from Friday.'

'You still want to go to Ikea?' He sent her a sideways look.

'Yes, if only for visual ideas.'

He shrugged. 'If you say so.'

'I do.' She laughed at the expression of doubt on his face. 'Trust me.'

The corners of his mouth turned up before he said, 'I will.'

'In the meantime, search Swedish Christmas decor for me.' She tapped the laptop screen.

He frowned.

'I need to know what to expect so I don't become distracted tomorrow by things you don't like.'

'I like your taste.'

She tilted her head and studied him.

'I have watched you work in the hotel and in the classes and I have seen your home.'

'True.' She put the mug of tea down. 'Let's see this spreadsheet then.'

'As you wish.' His eyes danced and she had second thoughts about spending more time with him. With each passing minute she found him more attractive instead of discovering things she didn't like about him. But she would find a way to keep her distance even if it was simply all the work that needed to be done in such a short time.

Chapter Eleven

Monday, they had made it in and out of Ikea, buying only the items that fit the remit – white fairy lights, red and green ribbon and simple clear glass ornaments and red ones. It was Theo's plan to carefully fill the clear ones with foliage. Last night she had sketched out the trees and planned the decorations for the various fireplaces. She raided her stash of dried hydrangea heads and teasels. The latter she would give a light spray of silver paint. That, together with the foliage, should do it. Blending the two cultures should be easy. It would be good if Tim could lend them a hand when they reached the finishing stages. With all the painting it would take all the hours that she had available.

It was still dark when Theo arrived at Gwen an Hal this morning. Her breath clouded around her as she looked up at the last stars still filling the sky. She walked through the walled kitchen garden pausing to think of what she could do with it. Warm light fell through the glass extension to the kitchen.

Her phone pinged. Tim's name flashed on the screen. He was freshening the hotel flowers today for her, freeing up more time.

How's it going my lovely? You and Erik loved up yet? Thought I might pop round later and see how the house is coming on.

Theo bit her lip. Part of her wanted to throttle him and the other hug him. An extra pair of hands would speed things up no end if he had the time.

Do come, and wear clothes to paint in.

She pressed send before opening the back door where she was greeted with the smell of coffee and Christmas spices. Her stomach tightened and it wasn't from hunger. Erik stood barefoot in the kitchen wearing faded jeans and a blue T-shirt that matched the colour of his eyes.

'What are you baking?' She put her bag down.

'Pepparkakor again, to keep our energy levels up today.'

'It smells divine, as does the coffee.'

He picked up the cafetière and poured her a cup. 'Have you had breakfast?'

'Yes, a bit of yoghurt and a piece of toast.'

'Is that enough?' He held her glance.

'It is.' She reached into her coat pocket and rubbed the ears of Zach's rabbit.

'I have made a chicken and vegetable soup for lunch.'

'You're spoiling the help.' She picked up a gingerbread biscuit not long out of the oven.

He laughed. 'No, just making sure you don't escape.'

'Not leaving until the job is done.' She popped half the biscuit into her mouth where it practically melted.

'I may have to slow you down then.' He hid his expression behind his cup but his eyes sparkled.

'Never,' she replied, taking off her coat. 'Let's get to work. Dining room?'

'Yes.'

She picked up her coffee cup and followed him to the dining room where she opened the windows. No matter how good the quality of the paint, a day spent breathing it was never ideal. Despite the cold air, she pushed up the sleeves of her old canvas work smock and picked up a paint roller. Erik worked the top half of the walls while she did the lower. In the background, Christmas music played through the high-tech sound system wired through the house. Before long they had given two of the walls a second coat. They worked together, almost like they were partnering in a dance.

She stood back to admire their work and rubbed her lower back.

'Time for a break,' he said, putting his brush safely in a tub.

'Good idea.'

Erik collected her roller and placed it with his brush before heading into the kitchen. Theo followed and enjoyed watching him move with such confidence about the kitchen. Everything she discovered about him was appealing and this was dangerous. She stopped by the central island where the Christmas biscuits sat, picked one up, and sniffed in the delicious aroma.

'They aren't poisoned,' he said making coffee. 'I promise.'

'You can't afford to kill off the help.'

'Too right and why would I want to kill a beautiful woman?'

Theo looked down. Once she was beautiful once but now she was a grandmother and beauty wasn't a requirement. This had been a relief but standing here with Erik she wanted to be beautiful for him. This was something she hadn't felt for years. She looked across the counter at Erik and her breath caught. This was a dangerous game. Her life had a hard-won equilibrium. Yes, she was a bit lonely at the moment but that was a matter of adjustment. But those blue eyes promised something more than filling her loneliness. Was she ready for that? No, certainly not.

He handed her a mug of coffee and she smiled her thanks, quickly glancing down in case he could read her thoughts. It was best to focus on the goal of delivering Christmas for Erik and his son and leave this silly nonsense of desire and the heady feeling of being wanted where it belonged – not in her life. She was enough and Erik, she knew, would not be short of willing partners although from what he had said he had been lost in grief for years.

'Shall we try and finish in the dining room before we stop for lunch?' she asked, pushing her wayward thoughts aside.

He grinned. 'You are a hard taskmaster but yes, that is a good plan.'

'It's a week until Christmas Eve.'

He drew a deep breath. 'Time is going too quickly.'

'You're the reverse of a child counting the minutes until Christmas arrives.'

'I'm enjoying the lead up to the holiday too much.' He paused. 'Because of you.'

Theo swallowed. 'Thank you.' She put her mug in the sink. 'Now let's get back to work because no matter what we want, we only have seven days.' And right in that moment Theo knew exactly what she wanted for Christmas and she needed to make sure she didn't get it.

Chapter Twelve

Theo started the engine. She had been lucky to be able to open the car door. In her three winters living at Boatman's, she had only ever experienced a light frost. This morning she had woken to Cat burrowing under the duvet and the world covered in a thick coat of ice. Despite the freezing temperature, the car started on the second attempt. It would take at least half an hour to begin to defrost.

She picked her way across the frozen ground. It was bright and breathtaking but bloody brass monkeys as her father used to say, much to her mother's disapproval, which had made Theo use the expression whenever she could. Cat hadn't even bothered to venture forth after breakfast but returned to the comfort of Theo's bed. If it wasn't the last day to help Erik, Theo would be tempted to do the same. But it was Christmas Eve and Erik's son was due around five, traffic permitting. By then she would be back here with Cat and the finest ready-made Christmas food that could be bought.

Last night, after much persuasion, she agreed to go and join the in-laws at David's on Boxing Day for a walk and a bite to eat. It interrupted her days of doing nothing but it would be fine because she had tonight and all day tomorrow to recover from her week of non-stop work with Erik. She had enjoyed every minute of it, even if her aching muscles told a different story.

Her breath clouded in front of her. At least it was lovely and warm in Boatman's and so would her car be in a bit. Inside while she waited for the coffee to brew, she opened her computer and checked her emails. Tim had been on top of all the business stuff which he'd promised. Thankfully this time of year was normally quiet once the Christmas prep was finished. She ignored his cheeky query about how things were going with the hot Swede and instead thanked him for his help. Tim had devoted many hours to helping them complete the painting.

She leaned back. Over the past few days, Erik's sadness that Oskar would be selling the house became apparent. She would be sad too. He had put so much work, so much love, into it. It was far more than decorating; it was his way of showing his son his love for him. She could only hope that Oskar would see it.

She plunged the coffee and buttered a piece of toast. The computer pinged and she glanced at the screen. Toby had sent an email. No doubt it was another plea to come and spend Christmas with him.

Putting her mug down she nibbled the toast and scanned the contents. It wasn't what she thought at all.

Theo,
Happy Christmas. I won't pressure you to come and join us again. You know you are welcome. Other than sending Christmas greetings I wanted to share my mother's diary entry with you. I've attached photos of the pages. She wrote about meeting you and your grandmother. I thought you'd like to know that she had made the connection. But I won't say more, I'll let you read it for yourself.
See you in the new year, if not before.
Love,
Toby

Theo opened the first photo.

20th July, 1971

    Today was the most extraordinary day and I can't quite settle because my heart is joyous. The gardens were open and we raised one hundred and twenty pounds for the children's welfare charity which is our highest total yet. But that is not what has me so restless. Today Claire Pascoe came to the garden. She had said she had wanted to for years but hadn't been ready to. She is a beautiful and proud woman and I can see why my John had fallen for her. Beside her was John's granddaughter, Theodora, and she was the image of me as a child, but much much calmer. While she raced after a butterfly and met up with Constance who told her all about them, I found out about my family, the one I didn't know I had. Claire's son Thomas was a vicar in a parish in Gloucestershire and his wife Virginia had just given birth to their second child, a son. Claire brought Theodora to Cornwall every year to give her son and daughter-in-law a break and to have an excuse to return.

    I asked her about her parents and she turned away. I didn't think she would say any more, but she did. She told me that she had seen them once after Thomas was born. I took her hand in mine. Thousands of questions ran through my mind but I couldn't ask them. I had to wait and even now I struggle with that. Only after Theodora had come back to us for permission to see the fish pond with Constance did Claire say more.

    When she lost John and knew she was pregnant she couldn't go home. They wouldn't have understood and they would have made her give up her child. So she had Thomas and went north pretending to be a war widow. There she worked as a matron in a school. She had never received my letter which I knew when it had been returned. We would have given her and Thomas the home that John wanted for them.

When my beautiful great-granddaughter came back we walked in silence for a while through the garden. I had to ask – for she was a very young woman when John died – I needed to know. It came out of me in a muddle of words. And she said no, she had never loved anyone else again. Her son and his children were her life.

That is why I am so restless. John would have wanted her to love again and love fully. I have loved twice and for that I am grateful. I am also restless because I long to meet my grandson. She didn't ask me not to contact him but it was in her eyes. To him she is a war widow, and in truth that is who she is. In all but certificate she is Claire St Loy. They had made their promises to each other. She tried to give me the emerald ring. It hung about her neck. I told her it was hers for she had given her heart to John and he had loved her. It had been his to give and so much more.

I think she had come to the gardens to try and give me the ring, that and curiosity. She said that John looked like me and he did. She said his son, Thomas, was the image of John, and it was clear to see myself in Theodora. So many memories of love were and are with me.

I don't know what to do other than to pray for the family that is mine but must never know it. Yet I long to bring them into the fold so that they may know each other. Enough words for today. It is time to go onto my knees and to pray for them all. Mostly I want to pray that Claire lets love into her life again. It is never too late.

Theo closed her eyes. Alice knew. Gran knew. Theo lifted

the ring from her chest and played with it as she opened the next picture.

19th December, 1971

He looks so like John and even sounds like him. His sermon on this fourth Sunday of advent was excellent and I found myself weeping at the back of the church. I wept for my son and the son he hadn't known. I wept for myself. So much loss and there was nothing I could do. I couldn't change things. I couldn't bring John back and I couldn't destroy the artifice that Claire had created just because I wanted my grandson.

He found me weeping. Without a word he sat and waited until the tears had stopped then proffered me his clean hankie. His hands were John's, his eyes were a little lighter but the smile. That was like it came straight from heaven. But the man I was looking at was older than John had been when I'd last seen him.

He spoke quietly and asked if I needed water or a chat. I refused both. Then he said that at moments like these when it all feels too much, he looks at the cross and realises that sometimes love asks so much of you but it's worth it. He took my hand in his and looked me directly in the eyes. In that moment he saw something for he squeezed my hand and said sometimes love asks for silence. I nodded. Then he added, but even without words love is felt and shared. He stood, releasing my hand, then he bent down and rested his cheek against mine and whispered I know who you must be, thank you for coming. He took my hand once more, briefly, then disappeared.

Theo read the passage again, not believing the words, but why would Lady Alice write it if it wasn't true? Surely her father hadn't known but this says he had. Theo had been six when she had met Alice, and Theo looked so like her. Something inside her settled despite the dampness on her cheeks. Love had found a way.

Theo ran her fingers over the keyboard, she typed that she could not find the words to express the emotions inside her and she sent her love to all the family. Once the computer was shut down she added a little extra food for Cat in case she left the comfort of her bed. When Theo returned later Cat would have fresh salmon for dinner. It was Christmas Eve and she had a great deal of work in front of her if Erik was going to deliver a Christmas to his son. She hoped Oskar would see how hard Erik had worked and that might just open a crack big enough so that love would find a way in again.

* * *

'Merry Christmas Eve,' Tim said.

'Bah humbug.' Theo kissed his cheek.

'Still feeling Grinchy even with all that time you've spent with the hot Swede, or is he a turnip in disguise?'

Theo coughed.

'Don't tell me after all the hours you have spent with this man you haven't so much as snogged him?'

Theo pressed her lips together. She had thought about it, but each time they had come close she had stopped.

'You disappoint me. I never would have put you down as chicken, but you are.'

'Cluck, cluck.'

'Bloody hell woman, it's Christmas Eve! Find yourself some mistletoe and your courage. At least kiss him.'

'That's not sensible.' She placed her hands on her hips.

'Since when is lust or Christmas sensible? And the two together is a licence to thrill or be thrilled!'

'Enough. I have said before, I am not lonely.'

'Of course you're not lonely, you've been with the hot Swede.'

Theo blushed. 'Would you stop calling him that!'

'Absolutely not, because it's true and because it unsettles you.'

Theo put her hands up. She was never going to win this one. 'Where's the box of cuttings?'

'Changing the subject?' He raised an eyebrow.

'Absolutely. I haven't a chance of winning this argument with you.'

'Finally, you see the light.' He began walking to the garden wall. 'And if you know what is good for you, kiss him at minimum. Give yourself that kiss to build a dream on for your solo Christmas Eve.'

Theo stuck her tongue out at him.

'It's not me that needs to see that sass but Erik.'

'You don't let up.'

He thrust a large box into her hands and grabbed another one. 'Absolutely not, and have you seen a picture of this Oskar? Does he look like his dad?'

She walked to her car and placed the box in the boot. 'I'd say he's better looking.'

'There, you admit that Erik is hot.' Tim placed the second box in the boot.

Theo smirked. 'Never denied it.'

'Drive carefully.' He pulled her into a hug. 'The weather is set to get worse.'

'I know.'

'Do you have enough food in? I don't want you and Cat starving and alone over the holidays if we get snowed in.'

'I do.' She opened the driver's side door of the car.

'Good, being alone is bad enough.'

She crossed her arms. 'I have Cat and I like my own company.'

'I'm sure but I imagine Erik is better than any toy you may have at home.'

Theo opened her eyes wide, not sure she'd heard correctly what Tim had just said.

He winked. 'Just saying, and there is only one way to find out.'

'The cheek of you!' She said tapping him on the arm.

'Go for it. You have nothing to lose.'

'It's never as easy as that.' Theo kissed his cheek and climbed into her car. The temperature was dropping and the rain was almost sleet like. It would make for tricky driving and she would need to be careful.

Chapter Thirteen

Theo let the car go with the skid before bringing it back under control. Another car had taken out the telephone pole on the other side of the road. The black ice covering most of the road surface was treacherous and would only become worse as the day wore on. Everything in her told her to turn around and head home while she could, but instead she crept along the roads. In fact she focused entirely on the road and not the reason she was still going. It was easier to drive than to think.

'Whoa,' she said, viewing the front end of a car in a phone junction box in the village nearest to Oskar's house. That was not what people needed on a holiday when people tried to connect with others.

She turned off the paved road and onto the track that led to the house and the driving became a bit easier. It was still slippery but there were no other cars and the ruts and the gravel gave the wheels something other than ice to hold onto. But the puddles had frozen over. The temperature must have dropped to below zero and it might be wishful thinking, but the rain looked white.

By the time the house was in view, she was certain it was snow and she should simply deliver the greenery and turn around. If she didn't she might become stranded and she might do something reckless. A little voice in her head said she already had by not turning around earlier. She argued back to the little voice that she hadn't known the roads would be this bad so she had been sensible and she didn't want to let Erik down.

The car skidded to a halt and Theo took a deep breath. The scent of fir, yew and cedar cuttings had escaped the boot and filled her lungs. It was Christmas Eve and it was snowing. What could be bad about that?

Erik opened the back door with concern written across his face. 'I tried to ring you to tell you to not to come.'

'You've finished without me?' Theo stood in the falling snow.

'No, of course not. I was worried about you but the phones are out and the internet is down.'

He had been worried about her. She let that sink in. 'There was an accident that had taken out a telephone pole and another car had skidded into the junction box thing.'

He looked out at her car.

'Both the car and I are fine but others aren't so lucky.' She opened the boot and Erik joined her, taking the largest box. She grabbed the smaller box then closed the boot.

Once she was inside the warm bright kitchen, and the boxes were down, she relaxed. It had been a more fraught journey. She hung her coat and took a deep breath. The kitchen smelled of cinnamon, cloves and ham. 'I almost turned back but I'm glad I made it.'

'I am too.' He held his hand above his head.

'What on earth are you doing?'

'Trying to get phone signal so I can tell Oskar to take care.'

Theo laughed. Signal here was awful at the best of times. 'It might be easier to drive down the lane a bit. My phone normally springs to life by the big boulder and the oak tree.'

He grabbed his jacket. 'Good thinking. Make yourself at home.'

Theo already had a mug in hand and was heading for the coffee pot. She did feel very at home here but that wasn't a surprise. She had worked on every room in the house in some way or other. With her coffee in hand, she wandered into the sitting room. The white lights on the tree sparkled and the ornaments were ready for Erik and Oskar to decorate this tree themselves. Sadly not as Erik would have wished, the day before Christmas Eve, but at least they could do it together. That was what was important. Meanwhile she and Erik would trim the tree in the kitchen, and she would finish the fireplaces and the hallway while Erik worked on the food. Erik and Oskar would have a Christmas to remember, and she would be home with Cat by six at the latest. There was salmon, champagne and *A Christmas Carol* for her in front of the fire. Bliss.

A trail of cold air around her ankles alerted her to Erik's return. When she joined him in the kitchen, he was taking a tray out of the oven. 'Message sent I think, and I'll drive or walk down there later to see if I have a reply.'

'What is that?' Theo studied the S shaped buns.

'Lussekatter, a type of saffron bun usually eaten on St Lucia's day.'

'Smells wonderful.'

'I hope so.' He half smiled. 'Today is the big day.'

'Oskar will love it.'

He nodded but didn't appear convinced. 'It could all backfire.'

Theo walked to his side and placed a hand on his arm. 'Love is never straightforward but always worthwhile.' As she said the words she thought of Alice.

He put his hand over hers and said, 'Thank you.' He leaned forward and kissed her cheek. He smelled of the cold air outside and the warm saffron buns. She closed her eyes for a moment. It would be so easy to turn her head and kiss him, kiss him properly. Instead she smiled and pulled back.

'Right we only have a few hours left to finish.' She took one of the boxes of greenery and headed into the sitting room to adorn the fireplace. She set her phone down and put on a Christmas play list. Without working Wi-Fi the sound system in the house didn't connect. Everything depended on technology these days. She was grateful she'd downloaded several Christmas playlists onto her phone for the dead spots she would frequently drive through. Nothing was worse than a sound cutting out when you were enjoying it.

While she hummed along to the carols, she covered the fireplace in fir branches, holly and ivy. She stepped back to check the balance and nearly fell over. Erik's arms caught her. She hadn't heard him come in. Once steady on her feet, he didn't drop his hands but stood still looking over her shoulder at her work. 'Beautiful.'

She turned her head then stopped. He was so close again and if she swivelled further she would be fully in his embrace.

'Thank you,' she whispered.

His breath caressed the side of her neck and she shivered, but not from the cold. It was imagining his mouth on the sensitive skin by her ear. She pulled herself together and stepped towards the window. It was snowing properly. The ground was covered in a dusting of white. The bright green grass and the dark stones in the low garden wall jumped out in contrast.

'It's mesmerising to watch.' He came and stood beside her.

'It is but there is work to do and not many hours in the day.'

'The food is prepared so I can now give you a hand in the dining room and the hall.'

She bent to pick up the box. With the rate of snowfall she had better work fast. 'Great.'

She handed the box to Erik and sent him to the dining room while she detoured to collect the other box. The kitchen tree lights sparkled and it didn't need decoration but she loved doing it. They could quickly finish the rest of the house and focus on the tree. Theo glanced at her watch. It was already one o'clock. She raced into the dining room.

* * *

Darkness had come early with the snow. They had completed everything except placing the star on the kitchen tree. The sense of accomplishment was good, but she was also sad to have finished the task and to have no reason to linger any longer. She climbed the small step stool. Erik held her waist as she reached to place the star on the top of the tree. His hands were a safety measure, but it felt like more. A wave of longing filled her as his hand slipped onto the bare skin where her jumper met her jeans.

'Done,' she said, coming down the ladder.

His hands remained in place as she turned to face him.

'Thank you for all your help.'

'I've loved doing it.'

They stood under the mistletoe. When he hung it earlier in the day, he told her the story of how Oskar had met his husband at a Christmas party and they had kissed under the mistletoe. Erik was convinced that was one of the reasons that Oskar ignored Christmas, and she sensed his uncertainty about his son's reaction to the holiday.

With a sigh she looked out at the snow. There were at least two inches on the ground which should be fine as long as there wasn't ice under it. 'I best head off now.'

'You will be careful.'

'I will.'

'If Oskar wasn't due then I would drive you back,' he said. 'I have a bit more experience of driving in the snow.'

'True.' She couldn't delay her departure any longer so she

put her hat and coat on. When she turned Erik was still standing under the mistletoe. His gaze was fixed outside at the snow. She walked up to him. It was Christmas Eve and one kiss would not change anything. She tiptoed and kissed him. 'Merry Christmas,' she whispered.

'Merry Christmas,' he said and kissed her. His mouth lingering a moment longer on hers. She could smell the pepparkakor he'd eaten a few minutes ago and she wanted to kiss him again. This was dangerous. Like the gingerbread biscuits, one kiss or even two was not enough. She had forgotten how good it felt. She drew a breath and stepped away.

'The roads won't be improving so I'd better go.'

He grabbed his coat and walked out to the car with her. She turned the engine on and joined him clearing the snow off the windows. Before she could overthink it, she made a snowball and threw it, hitting him in the chest. His retaliation was swift and his hit her in the stomach. She slipped and landed ungracefully on her backside. He came rushing to her side.

'So sorry,' he said, holding out a hand to help her up. Instead of taking it she lay back on the ground and began to make snow angels. She hadn't done this since she was fifteen and her family had been living in Northumberland.

Erik stretched out on the ground at arm's length and made his own. Their hands touched as they made their wings. Theo laughed, standing and brushing the snow off her jeans. She held out a hand to Erik. He took it and her heart flipped with the happiness in his eyes. He was really too attractive and she wanted to kiss him again, but she needed to head home to Cat, the champagne and the salmon, as planned.

'Let me know how it goes, please,' she said opening the car door.

'I will, once I can communicate with the world again.'

'Sometime in February then.'

He took her hand in his. 'Hopefully not that long. Please take the journey slowly.'

'I will.' She climbed in, waved to him and set off down the drive.

Theo coaxed the car along the track while the wheels kept slipping. There was more snow here than at the house and the earlier sleet had clearly iced over. When she came to the bend with the boulder and the oak tree, her car spun out and careened off the track and half into a ditch.

'Blast.' Her heart pounded. She put the car into reverse but the wheels spun, not gaining a purchase. Once out of the car, she saw why. Only the driver's side front wheel and the rear passenger wheel were on the ground. Under the snow it was sheet ice. She was going nowhere. At least her car was out of the way if a passing vehicle needed to get through. She closed her eyes. This was not how it was supposed to go. She had flirted outrageously with Erik and kissed him knowing that she was leaving. Now she was going to have to go back.

She sent a quick text to David saying she was stranded at a friend's on Bodmin and there was no signal at their house. A bitter north wind battered her as she typed and her fingers were going numb. After wishing them all a happy Christmas, she pressed send, grabbed her bag and her torch and headed back up towards the house as fast as the conditions would allow. Somehow she would manage this. After all she was a grown woman.

By the time she'd reached the house, she was cold through. Snow was caked to her clothing and she suspected her lips were blue. She was dressed for winter in Cornwall, not a skiing holiday.

Theo tapped on the door. Erik was by the stove and swung around. She must look like a ghost or a yeti at this point.

He raced to the door. 'Are you OK?'

Her teeth chattered an inherent reply.

'What happened?' He helped her out of the coat and hat. 'Go and stand by the fire.'

Theo couldn't speak, she was too cold and shock had finally set in. Erik rubbed her hands in his and slowly feeling came back into them. Only then he took a throw off the sofa and wrapped it around her before leading her to the armchair near the fire.

'The car?' he asked.

'Stuck,' she managed to say.

'I'm going to run you a bath.'

Theo watched him disappear. This was not the Christmas Eve she had planned. She was stranded with a handsome man alone. The biggest problem was that she wasn't upset about this and she should be. At least she had left extra food down for Cat and she knew that the feline was safe, if frustrated, at being stuck inside. So she simply needed to relax. She wasn't ruining anyone's plans because she doubted if Oskar would be able to make it this far, and for that she was sorry. Erik had so wanted this Christmas Eve to be special for him. But the weather, it appeared, had other plans. She wriggled her toes and she began to feel them again.

'It's all ready for you in the main front bedroom.' He smiled. 'I've put out some pyjamas for you and we can put your clothes into the dryer.'

She stood and headed slowly up the stairs, seeing the blazing fire and the tree sparkling. From the landing window, the falling snow was highlighted by the light by the front door. It was the perfect Christmas scene.

True to his word the bath was ready. Erik had lit a candle and left some bath salts by the side. She wasn't used to being this spoiled. Once she had peeled off her wet jeans, she immersed herself in gloriously hot water.

She might have dropped off because she flinched when she heard Erik knocking on the door.

'All OK in there?'

She sat upright. 'Yes, thank you.'

'Good. I walked down to your car. You were lucky.'

'I was.'

'I sent another message to Oskar but I don't think he'll make it.' He paused. 'The weather forecast is getting worse, not better.'

'I'm so sorry.' She exhaled. This must be such a disappointment.

'It's not your fault.'

'I know, but you've worked so hard.'

'It will all still be here when he arrives. But I won't disturb your bath any longer.'

Theo listened to his footsteps on the wide plank floors. Once she couldn't hear them anymore, she quickly washed her hair, left the bath, and blew out the candle. She laughed when she caught sight of herself in the mirror. The PJs were too big and made her look like one of the lost boys of *Peter Pan* fame, if they were middle-aged.

She found a hairdryer in the bathroom cupboard and used the socket in the bedroom. She didn't need to style it but it wouldn't do if she went around with wet hair, because she had been chilled enough earlier. Her hair was almost done when everything was plunged into darkness. She picked up her phone to use the torch to make her way downstairs.

Candles were alight in the kitchen but there was no sign of Erik. Outside she spied the light of his torch and in the kitchen she noticed the fuse box open. The house was still very warm but she knew the system was complicated involving ground source heating and solar power. Something scratched at the

98

back of her mind that some outside electric was required. Had another poor soul come amok on the roads and taken down a power line?

Erik shook the snow from his hair when he returned with oil lamps in his hands.

'The problem is not in the house. But at least we have these.' He lifted the lamps. 'And the wood burners, so we will be warm enough and can see where we are going.'

'I didn't expect to be snowed in on Christmas Eve.'

'I didn't either but I can't think of another person I'd rather be with.' He looked directly at her and Theo steadied herself on the counter.

'Me either,' she said and she meant it. She would relax and enjoy this unusual time, even if she was in his pyjamas and out of her depth.

Chapter Fourteen

The candlelight cast moving shadows on the white painted panelling. Outside was the eerie luminescent light of snow in the moonlight. The snow had stopped an hour ago and the sky had cleared. The landscape was all the shades of white, grey, purple, and blue. The snow had settled thickly and with amazing speed. She could be in the mountains and not on a Cornish moor. All the features picked out by the moon had a sharpness. Where the stones weren't covered their shapes were black and defined. It was Christmas Eve and not the one she had been expecting. She hoped that Cat was OK. At least Theo knew she was inside. The feline would have to wait until Christmas Day for more food. Of course, that assumed a thaw of some sort, but the weather reports varied depending on which way this particular cold front would go.

She turned from the window and the view. Erik was singing a song she didn't recognise in the kitchen. He had fully charged his phone in his car and that was their only functioning bit of technology, except her own phone. Now for better or worse she was not spending Christmas alone. She was in the company of a very attractive man.

She paused on the threshold to the kitchen. Was she at a crossroads? For the past two weeks they had been flirting. He'd made his interest clear. Did she take a chance? He stood, unaware of her thoughts, by the centre island bathed in the light of old oil lamps. In front of him was an impressive spread of cold foods and a bottle of champagne.

He looked up and a slow smile appeared on his face. There was only one thing she had to lose and that was her dignity. With three long steps, she was at his side. Why did she need dignity when she was stranded with an attractive man, a bottle of champagne and no place to go?

His glance met hers. 'Are you hungry?'

'Yes, very.' She didn't look away. She was an adult who knew what she wanted.

'Good.' He opened a bottle of schnapps. His fingers touched hers as he gave her a glass. She shivered in anticipation.

'This is traditional with sill.' He waved his hand towards the platter covered with fish.

'Happy Christmas.' She raised her glass and met his glance.

'God Jul, indeed.' He said, then he took a sip with his eyes never leaving her. He took the platter and cutlery while she grabbed the napkins and plates. Together they walked through to the sitting room. They both placed the things down and together they pulled the smaller sofa closer to the fire.

As Erik returned to the kitchen for the champagne, he stumbled on the box of ornaments and his face fell. He had so looked forward to finishing the tree with his son. She pulled the box closer to the tree and in the low light of the fire she looked at the array of ornaments. Most of them were handmade and she guessed many were made by Oskar. She had kept all those that David had made over the years, from the glitter covered Christmas trees to the play dough baked gold star. Those years passed so quickly.

Hearing Erik's footsteps returning, she sat on the sofa. The warmth of the fire was needed because the temperature had dropped further outside, and the heat pump wasn't working without the electricity.

He sat beside her and asked, 'Do you like herring?'

Theo shrugged. 'I've never tried it.'

'You are in for a treat.' He poured the champagne. 'I suggest you try a little of everything.'

Theo hesitated but chastised herself. It was only fish, which she loved.

'This one is pickled with Christmas spices,' He put a small piece on her plate. 'And last year I tried this one using whisky, which I loved.' He added that to her plate. 'What do you have on Christmas Eve?'

'Growing up it was fish pie but this year I planned on a salmon fillet.'

'There is salmon. Gravadlax.'

'You were making that earlier this week.'

'I was.'

Theo tried the fish on her plate, surprised by the flavours, and the texture was far better than she feared. She then helped herself to the gravadlax. 'Tell me about your Christmases.'

'It's always been about Christmas Eve which means food, family and friends.'

'For us that's Christmas Day.' She shook her head. 'For years I was running ragged on Christmas Eve just to have everything ready.' She took a sip of her champagne. 'When I was growing up it was such a busy day for my father, we wouldn't sit down as a family until early evening.'

'I forgot you were the vicar's daughter and that your brother is a priest and a physicist.'

Theo laughed. 'He was always going to be different and difficult.'

'Sibling rivalry?'

'Not really, he was just the annoying younger brother.'

'What about you?' she said.

'I am the annoying older brother.' He topped up her glass of champagne.

'Are your sisters missing you?'

He tilted his head. 'I imagine so but they are worried about Oskar too.' He glanced at his phone. 'I keep hoping that we will have signal and I will hear from him.'

'Understandable.' She reached out and touched his hand. 'Hopefully he is safely tucked up in a hotel, or maybe in view of the weather he stayed put in London.'

'Probably the latter.' Erik played with his phone and put on some Christmas music. 'Would you care to dance?'

Theo looked down at the pyjamas. 'In these?'

'I'll have you know they are my best and in truth have never been worn.'

Theo raised an eyebrow.

'I don't sleep in pyjamas but I thought I'd better bring some in case Oskar surprised me and brought someone.'

Theo blinked, enjoying the image his words had created in her mind.

He stood. 'Dance?'

She took his hand and he pulled her into his arms, and they moved slowly to the dulcet tones of Michael Bublé. The champagne had definitely gone to her head because she moved her body closer to his and rested her head on his chest. Who was this woman? She didn't know, but the woman was enjoying herself.

He kissed her, and unlike the quick kisses under the mistletoe, these were deeper and were asking questions. Theo didn't know the answers.

She pulled back and looked at him. 'I'm not sure. I . . .'

'You?'

'I haven't been with anyone other than my ex in more than thirty years.'

He smiled. 'Maybe it's time to try with a new model?'

She took a deep breath and took his hand. All she had to lose was her dignity and she'd already spent the evening in his pyjamas.

Chapter Fifteen

Theo snuggled under the duvet and moved closer to Erik trying to hide from the light and the noise.

'Morning,' he said over the sound of the burglar alarm.

'Morning.' She blinked. The light in the room hadn't seemed too bright last night when she had a bath, but this morning it was blinding.

'I'd better go and reset the alarm. It appears electricity has been restored.'

'Merry Christmas,' she said.

'Merry Christmas.' He kissed her then slipped out from under the duvet. He found his jeans on the floor where they had landed last night. Theo blushed, remembering the hunger that had raced through her. Despite her years of enforced chastity, her body fully remembered what to do. After the initial fear which obviously the champagne had dulled, she relished feeling her body come back to life. Erik sent her a sexy smile as he met her glance. He came back and kissed her again.

'I'll make some coffee but please stay put.'

'Sounds good,' she said nestling under the duvet. She didn't have stitch on and couldn't remember the last time she had slept in the nude.

The alarm stopped and Theo closed her eyes for a moment. It was Christmas morning. Seven thirty to be precise. Outside was still dark but the sky was showing signs of brightening. She ached in places she had forgotten about, but she was content. Her dignity had been thrown out the window and yet she wasn't embarrassed. This was strange but her desire felt right, normal and needed. Erik had been kind, funny and passionate. So attentive to her needs that she had been shocked. The last time that had happened had been that one night in Paris. In fact, this morning she was closer to the young Theo than she had ever been since then. Last night she and Erik had made love once rather than multiple times, but she had felt more seen and more cared for. Was that what age brought to you? She laughed. Less stamina but more understanding on both sides?

Christmas music and the aroma of coffee drifted up from the kitchen. She could go and help, or she could just lie here and enjoy the moment. It may not happen again. After all, Erik was here solely to work on the house for his son. He talked of heading off sailing and that wasn't her life. Her life was in Boatman's, beside the Tamar, with Cat for company and flowers for inspiration. This moment was a Christmas gift. No one but Erik and her would ever know what had happened when they were stranded together. And people like them didn't do reckless things at their age. She blushed again. It had been so joyous and so imperfect that it had been perfect. Two fifty somethings writhing around and discovering each other like they were horny teenagers. God, thank goodness no one would know.

Erik's big grin arrived almost before he did with a tray. The aroma of the coffee was almost as seductive as he was in just his jeans. She hoped they would make love again before she would have to go and check on her car and try to get some signal for her phone so she could send someone to check on Cat.

He placed the tray on the bed. Coffee, orange juice, saffron buns called lussekattor and champagne. Well, she didn't have to go anywhere right away. She looked out the window and saw the ground was still covered in snow.

Erik slipped off his jeans and joined her under the duvet without disturbing the tray. Theo slid closer to give him some of her warmth.

'It will take a little while for the house to warm up again.'

'Does that mean we have an excuse to stay here under the duvet?'

His eyes danced with mischief as he looked at her. 'It's a good excuse but I can think of a better one.'

'I like your thinking.'

'Good. So coffee or champagne first?'

'Both?'

He poured her coffee. 'Do you want orange juice with your champagne?'

'Sounds lovely.' She broke off a bit of croissant because she was famished and not just for the food.

* * *

Erik lay on the bed with his hands tucked behind his head. It was nearly noon when Theo ventured out of bed, full of champagne and cuddles. She didn't dive for the discarded pyjamas which had been her first thought. This was who she was and he had spent the last hours convincing her thoroughly how much he enjoyed all of who she was.

In the bathroom, she glanced at both the tub and the huge shower. Although the tub was big, fitting them both in it would turn into a puzzle solving exercise. But the shower was a thing of beauty. She turned the tap and adjusted the temperature. Once it was perfect, she popped her head through the bedroom door and beckoned to Erik to come and join her.

His smile was wide when he took her hand and they both went under the steaming water. The combination of water and

Erik was intoxicating, much more so than the fizz she had consumed. Maybe Tim and even her great-grandmother Alice were right. It was good to venture back into the waters of relationships. If Erik was anything to go on then there could be someone out there who would respect her and excite her at the same time.

She took the soap, lathered it and rubbed her hands across Erik's chest loving the feel of him. He leaned against the wall and closed his eyes as her hands moved lower. His arousal was obvious and she loved that she was the cause. Slowly she pressed herself into him and before long they were making love. The sensations of Erik and the water were so intoxicating that she almost didn't hear the squeal. But she did. In the entrance to the bathroom, Tim stood next to a younger Erik. What was more concerning was that David's mother-in-law, Jane, was right behind them.

'Well done girl,' Tim said, looking her directly in the eye then he turned and shooed everyone out of the bathroom saying, 'We've seen enough here to know some of us have had the best Christmas ever, without a turnip in sight.'

Erik burst out laughing. Theo couldn't breathe. So much for not losing her dignity. The look on Jane's face said she had lost the plot along with all her respect. Theo's legs slowly gave way when the reality sunk in. Erik's son had witnessed them. Dear God, could this have been any worse? If she had momentarily allowed the thoughts that this relationship could have continued, it was now firmly dead. The only benefit was that David hadn't seen them.

Erik helped her to her feet and kissed her. 'It's fine.'

'How can you say that?'

'Because it's true.' He lifted her chin with a finger. 'We are two consenting adults.'

She couldn't argue with that, but Jane's face and Tim's glee. 'Your son . . . '

'Knows I'm human.' He turned off the water and took her hand, leading her to the towels. He kissed her without haste and so thoroughly she forgot everything for a moment until questions began sprouting like weeds in her head.

'How are they all here?'

'That is a very good question and I will go find out.' He kissed her again. 'You take all the time you need and I will retrieve your clothes from the tumble dryer.'

'God, I'd forgotten about that. It wouldn't do to appear in your pyjamas.'

'I would appreciate taking them off you again.' He grinned and she tossed a damp towel at him, laughing. At least she could laugh at the moment. She dreaded the thought of going downstairs. She didn't have any make-up that she could put on to hide under either.

Erik dressed and disappeared while Theo dried her hair.

There was a tap on the door. She hesitated not sure who was on the other side because it didn't sound like Erik. 'Yes.'

David poked his head around the door. 'Mum?'

'Come in.' She was wrapped in a thick white dressing gown sitting on the bed.

He held out her clothes to her, raising an eyebrow. 'How are you?'

'Excellent,' she said, and she was. Despite the lack of make-up, she was glowing.

He cast her a sideways glance. 'How long have you been having an affair?'

She coughed. 'Affair?'

'Relationship then?'

'If you mean how long have I been sleeping with Erik the answer would be since last night.'

'I didn't need to know that.'

'Well, you bloody well asked.'

He looked down at his hands. 'Why don't you get dressed?'

'I will, but tell me who else is downstairs other than Jane, Tim and Oskar.'

'Everyone.'

'What do you mean everyone?' Images of large crowds of friends and family filling the kitchen ran through her mind.

'When none of us had heard from you we gathered at Abbotswood where Tim was with Oskar.'

'Tim was with Oskar?'

'Yes, Oskar made it as far the A30 near the Broadwoodwidger exit when the weather made it impossible to go much further. Abbotswood was the only place he could find a room.'

'Why was Tim there?'

'He was having dinner with Hugo and Gayle and Jeannette and Louis.'

'Oh, dear God, are you telling me they are all downstairs?'

He nodded.

Her humiliation was complete. Her dignity was a thing of the past. She wanted to slip out of the house and lose herself on the moor, never to be seen again.

'We've all been out of our minds with worry. So this morning we went to Boatman's and found Cat alone and hungry.'

'Is she OK?'

'Fine.' He drew a breath. 'Your car wasn't there. When I reached Tim he mentioned that when he saw you last you were heading here. That's where we decided to search after I had called the police and the hospitals.

'Good God, no.' She ran a hand through her hair, letting all of this information sink in.

'Yes.'

Theo closed her eyes. 'Why is Jane here?'

'Darren is too.'

She put her head in hands. 'Why?'

'Well they didn't make it to us last night and were on their way when Natasha called them to tell them not to come.' He sighed. 'They were almost there and they just joined the convoy.'

'Convoy?' She dropped her hands.

'Yes.'

'Not the police as well.' She opened her eyes wide trying to take this all in.

'No.'

'One saving grace then.'

'I have called them to say we have found you.'

'Oh, that's good of you.' She played with the cord on the robe.

'Mum, we were worried sick imagining you frozen solid in some ditch, not shacked up shagging the hot swede.'

'Not you as well.' Theo shook her head back and forth. This was worse than she thought. It didn't take much imagination to picture the array of cars making their way here, all thinking the worst only to discover her alive and more than well. She burst out laughing.

David sent her a look but soon he was laughing too.

'Not exactly the Christmas you planned,' he said.

She pressed her lips together for a moment. 'Actually it was far better than I could have imagined.'

He raised his hand. 'No, Mum, no.'

She laughed even more. 'Go, I need to get dressed.' She stood, hugged him then gave him a shove out the door. She simply needed to own this because she had had the best Christmas Eve and Christmas morning of her life. It was up to her to enjoy the rest of the day because she hadn't done anything wrong and she needed to remember that.

Chapter Sixteen

Theo paused in the doorway to the kitchen, her throat dry. No matter how much she reminded herself she had done nothing wrong aside from turn everyone's Christmas upside down, there was no denying she had been discovered having sex in a shower by Oskar, Tim and David's mother-in-law. Nothing could make that palatable. She was certain that she had scarred them for life, and she had no idea how she could ever look any of them in the eye again. And Tim would be insufferable.

Everyone had a schnapps in hand and were helping themselves to gravadlax and what was left of the sill. Erik's eyes met hers as she entered the kitchen and her insides tightened. This was not what she had imagined the rest of the day to look like. But her grandson was here, making happy squeals with Oskar by the Christmas tree. Tim was pulling food out of the fridge and Cat was being fed salmon by Louis.

'We have a ham and I'm sure we can cobble together a feast for the day,' said Tim.

'Wait,' Jane exclaimed. 'I have a turkey.'

Natasha rounded on her mother. 'You have a turkey?'

Jane looked sheepish. 'You were so worried about cooking yours that I cooked one this morning just in case.'

'I can't believe you did that.' Natasha rolled her eyes.

'Well, you never would have known if you hadn't needed it. I didn't want your Christmas spoiled.' Jane looked down and Theo's heart went out to her.

'Oh Mum.' Natasha gave her mother a hug. 'Christmas isn't about the turkey.'

'It smelled great on the journey,' said her father, Darren. 'It's probably still warm. I'll just go and get it.'

'My car is full of food too,' said Hugo, looking up. He spied Theo in the doorway and he winked. Theo paled. They all knew.

'Plus there's a case of pinot noir that will be perfect with that turkey,' Hugo added.

Theo gathered up her courage and asked, 'Why?'

'Why what?' Hugo headed towards the back door.

Theo cleared her throat. 'Why did you have a case of wine in your car?'

'Because it had arrived at the cottage instead of the hotel and I was bringing it to the hotel when the search party was formed.' He slipped out the door and Gayle grinned at Theo.

Erik took her hand and brought her fully into the room then gave her a schnapps. 'It's all good. We shall have a feast.'

'So you made snow angels?' Jeanette said, coming to her side.

Theo knew that was not what she was referring to at all but decided to ignore the insinuation. 'Yes, before I left and skidded off the track.'

'How fortunate. Things have turned out marvellously.' She picked up a glass of champagne. 'I can spend my favourite holiday with my favourite people. There's nothing better. We have good food, good wine and Oskar tells me there are enough beds that we won't have to worry about driving.'

Theo looked from Jeanette to Oskar. It was clear she had cast a spell over him as she had over everyone else. The only person missing from this array was Martin. He would love this strange blend of people.

Hugo and Darren arrived back inside with the turkey and the wine. Theo's phone on the countertop pinged with a thousand messages now that the Wi-Fi had returned. The last one was from Martin.

> I'm outside your cottage. Where the hell are you? Everyone's worried about you.

Theo swiftly typed.

> I'm at a friend's house on Bodmin moor and everyone else is too.

David came to her side. 'I've just sent Martin the postcode.'

Theo laughed. 'Next you'll tell me your grandmother is on the way.'

'No, she's with her new boyfriend.'

'Oh.'

'She is having a whale of a time.' David sent her a reproachful look. 'It's time both of you made up your differences.'

Theo swallowed. 'True. I suppose as it's Christmas I could take the first step.'

David hugged her.

She took a deep breath and opened a new message to her mother.

> Happy Christmas. Hope all is well with you. Would love to meet up in the new year. Love

Theo deleted love then typed it again

> Love, Theo

She pressed send before she could change her mind.

She had only just returned her phone to her pocket when the reply came.

> Happy Christmas to you. I would love that.
> Love, Mother

Tears welled in her eyes. This was a Christmas miracle. She couldn't recall the last time her mother had used the word 'love' with her. She glanced up to see Tim and Oskar standing side by side with Zach perched on Oskar's hip. The looks between the two of them spoke of a chemistry that made Theo's heart swell.

Erik came to her side and handed her a glass of champagne. His glance followed hers to his son.

'He always wanted kids and Zach is reminding him of what he had forgotten, as is Tim. I had hoped to introduce them but I'm happy they have done it themselves.'

Just then the back door opened and Martin walked in carrying a box of presents and what looked like a Christmas pudding. She was beginning to think they had all planned Christmas this way. She looked about all of them. Were they complicit? She couldn't believe that was the case, thinking of how they were discovered but as she saw the twinkle in both Tim and Martin's eyes she had to wonder.

'David, do you have Zach's bear?' Natasha asked.

He stopped mid step. 'No, I thought you did?'

She shook her head. 'He'll never take a nap without it.'

David's face fell. Theo's heart went out to him then she raced to her coat hanging by the door and pulled the small rabbit from it. She went to Natasha. 'Do you think this will work?'

Natasha's shoulders dropped down as she took the stuffed animal from Theo. 'Yes, it will.' She looked Theo in the eyes. 'You've just saved Christmas. Thank you.'

Jane came up to them and Theo wanted to run and hide.

'Merry Christmas.' She lifted her glass in a small salute. 'I'm pleased to see you moving on, Theo.'

Theo blinked.

'That takes courage.' Jane patted her arm.

Natasha kissed her cheek and went to take Zach for his nap with rabbit. Theo's glance met Oskar's. He walked towards her and she took a deep breath.

'Thank you for helping my father with the house.'

Theo opened her mouth then shut it again. What could she say?

'It looks wonderful, and I'm so pleased he convinced me to come back to Cornwall.'

Theo smiled. 'I am too.'

His eyes danced a bit like his father's. 'Yes, I can imagine.' He laughed and she joined him.

Tim brought over the bottle of champagne and refilled their glasses, looking from Oskar to Theo and back again. 'This has worked out better than I could have hoped.'

'It has.' Theo raised her glass. 'Happy Christmas.' She met Oskar's glance directly then Tim's before going in search of Erik.

'Shall we go and set the table in the dining room?' Erik asked. 'We should be able to fit everyone, and I can see that Tim and Jane have the food sorted.'

He took her hand and together they walked down the hall, listening to the happy chatter behind them. Once they were alone in the dining room Erik pulled her into his arms.

'This is the most unexpected but best Christmas ever.' He kissed her slowly.

When she could finally speak she said, 'Yes, simply the best.'

Author's Note

I love Christmas which made this story a joy to write. It has been such fun to spend time with Theo and her friends again. I just couldn't leave Theo after the end of *The River Between Us*. She stayed with me and encouraged me in a way to write this Christmas tale. I hope that it brings you a bit of Christmas cheer and laughter. It has for me.

If you are curious to discover how Theo Pascoe first found herself buying the run down Boatman's Cottage on the banks of the Tamar River then read her full story in my award winning novel, *The River Between Us*, published in 2021.

Acknowledgements

So many people help making a story shine. My wonderful Swedish editor Karolina Ek has been a huge support from the start. She too wanted Theo to find her happy ending. My writing buddies, the blessings - Brigid Coady and Deborah Harkness - brainstormed with me and Brigid read and reread the story many times. But it is my husband Chris who has been the star finding typos, researching, reading and simply putting up with me.

A huge shout out to my cover designed Berni Stevens, to my copy editor Laura Gerard and Anne Cater and her wonderful bloggers who have helped to spread the word about *Delivering Christmas*. If you've read this far and you loved Theo's story I'd be grateful for a review.

About the Author

Called *'the queen of the contemporary Cornish novel'* by the Guardian, Liz is the author of nine books and two novellas including the most recent book, *The Secret Shore*. She lives with her husband and two mad cats near the Helford River in Cornwall. When not writing Liz is reading, painting, knitting and procrastinating on social media.

Her books are available in English, Swedish, Dutch, German, Portuguese, French, Estonian, Norwegian, Danish, Turkish, Latvian, Serbian, Czech, Hungarian, Italian and Finnish.

If you would like to subscribe to Liz's newsletter, sign up via her website at lizfenwick.com.

Follow Liz Fenwick on:

facebook.com/liz.fenwick

x.com/@liz_fenwick

instagram.com/liz_fenwick

tiktok.com/@lizfenwickauthor

pinterest.com/lizfenwick3

Printed in Great Britain
by Amazon

33939396R00078